Greaveburn

Craig Hallam

Inspired Quill Publishing

Published by Inspired Quill: August 2012

First Edition

Contact the author through their website: www.craighallam.wordpress.com

Chief Editor: Peter Stewart
Typeset by ReallyLoveYourBook, Bridgend, South Wales

Paperback ISBN: 978-1-908600-12-7
eBook ISBN: 978-1-908600-13-4

Printed in the United Kingdom
1 2 3 4 5 6 7 8 9 10

Inspired Quill Publishing, UK
Business Reg. No. 7592847
http://www.inspired-quill.com

Dedication

To Laura.
Without her, this story would never have existed.

Acknowledgements

To everyone who made this possible. Editors, proof-readers, and Wombles. Friends who didn't roll their eyes when I talked about it *again* (James and Lindsey took the brunt of this, I think. Sorry guys). Matt, for constantly asking me when he could read it. Em and Ben, the southern contingent, who helped more than they realise. Marie, for spawning me in the first place. Don't blame her. She couldn't have known what she was about to unleash. Pete and Sue, for letting me vent in an author-friendly environment.

And all those who gave me ideas without even knowing it. You all outnumber me, and so more of your will has gone into this than my own.

Greaveburn

Part I

Rain pounded Greaveburn.

Rivulets coursed across acres of slate and through labyrinths of ornate stonework. Gurgling along gutters and rusty pipes, the torrent spewed into the narrow streets below, watched over by a tribe of gargoyles.

A cathedral to the Gods of despair and misery, the Citadel stood with its talons buried into the ancient cobbles. Water surged over its buttresses like the tendrils of a beast rising from the deep. Light spilled into the night from the great stained glass eye in its forehead, casting shadows across the square. Around the plaza, other buildings stood in the dark; slender demons with brickwork scales that watched the men below as if they were a meal wriggling on a platter.

Three guards in dripping uniforms stood over their prisoner as he knelt in the rising water, shivering from the cold and gnawing agony. Bruises blossomed across his face and neck like oil drops in water. More were visible through his cotton shirt, drenched through by the rain. His fair hair was streaked with blood and dirt. His breaths came in shudders.

Steadfast   stood   close   behind   his   prisoner.

Rainwater cascaded from the rim of his high-browed helmet, obscuring his features. He cupped the prisoner's forehead with one rough palm; a mother checking her child for fever. Lowering his mouth to the prisoner's ear, he whispered:

"Can you hear me, Darrant?"

A groan of confirmation, or agony, came from the prisoner. "I'm sorry, my friend, but The Duty comes first."

His sword scraped from its sheath. The prisoner tensed as its cold tip pressed against his back. Turning his head, Darrant rested his burning cheek against the damp material of Steadfast's uniform and gave another groan.

"I'll look after Greaveburn for you, and the girl, when I can. I'm going to release you and I don't want you to make a sound. Don't give them the satisfaction. Goodbye, my friend."

Steadfast's hand lowered from Darrant's brow to cover his mouth with tenderness.

"Not a sound now."

Darrant's body spasmed as the cold blade tore through flesh. His jaw dropped open, but no sound came. The rain rinsed dark crimson from the blade in gory streaks.

Darrant hit the cobbles, shallow breaths making bubbles in the rising water.

"Get rid of him."

With a sound like the scraping of tomb lids, a sewer cover was dragged aside.

Tipped head first into the abyss, Darrant's body disappeared into darkness. The following boom echoed through the sewers like the hoof beat of Death's steed.

1

P rofessor Loosestrife stood behind the lectern like a worm trapped in a jar. When he was finished decorating the chalk board with sweeping characters, he ran a hand over his high, polished head and down the lank white curtain that sprouted from behind his ears. Spinning on his heel, he presented himself to the audience.

"It can be *proven*," said Loosestrife, scratching the knuckle-like protrusion of his chin, "that the body consists of several base elements which, when separated from one another, are essentially useless. However, by combining said elements into a consumable form, it is conceivable that the medicinal benefits could far outweigh anything we have previously imagined."

And by *we*, he meant *them*. There was nothing that he couldn't imagine, no notion beyond his comprehension or objective too lofty for him to achieve.

He looked up into the gallery through eyebrows resembling ivy-encrusted balconies. Row upon row of alabaster faces stared back at him. Some of the audience shuffled under his gaze, averting the glowing discs of their spectacles. Starched collars were tugged at and neck ties were loosened, as if Loosestrife's eyes gave off heat.

"My friends," he continued, "if we could manufacture such an elixir, we would hold the very essence of life in the palm of our hands."

Raising his own hand, light reflected from the glove's rubber as if it were wet. Loosestrife ground the fingers closed and a high-pitched squeak escaped the fist.

No one seemed to notice.

"Such horrific-"

And perfect.

"-diseases such as The Ague, would be a thing of ancient history. Disease would be reduced to a tale to scare children before bedtime, a Bogeyman, a Boggle beneath the bed. Colleagues, we could turn this city of Greaveburn into a place of such splendour and perfection that the Gods themselves will sit up and take notice."

The last echoes of his voice drifted back to him and died. It had been a long lecture and many of the audience had ceased to pay attention hours ago. Loosestrife thought this could be the stuff of nightmares; row after row of pale faces staring down, emotionless.

"Thank you," he said, turning away from the lectern.

Bodies clambered toward the exit.

Loosestrife had already forgotten about them.

He stepped into the corridor that led to his office, his body visibly expanding as if shedding rusty manacles. Flicking hair from his shoulder, he stretched with a pop and crunch from his spine. His mind returned to the elixir.

Soon, he thought, *soon.*

Loosestrife ignored the door to his office. Instead, he prodded the corridor's wall with practiced certainty.

From somewhere inside came a hiss of compressed air. The wood panelling slid away.

The familiar musk of mouldering plaster made his nostrils flare.

Hanging his pristine lab coat on its hook inside the opening, he took down another covered with curious stains and smudges. Cobwebs stuck to his body like gossamer tattoos as he strode along the narrow corridor. Tugging off the long black glove on his right hand revealed a marvel; a cylindrical cage of brass rods replaced his forearm, the inner workings of which shifted as Loosestrife flexed his artificial hand. A series of amber plates made up his palm; fingers ended in tapered metal teardrops. He worked the fingers for a moment, basking in the perfection of his design.

The corridor's downward slope ended in an opening visible only as a darker rectangle in the gloom.

Loosestrife's shoes *pinged* and *doinged* as he moved out into the laboratory, and crossed its gridded metal floor. Six further levels extended into the abyss below, the lowest suspended over impenetrable darkness by wide chains which creaked under the tension.

The immense circular pit which held the laboratory had once been part of Greaveburn's ancient sewer system. Light drained from gratings above, turning green as it passed through mildew and mould. Weak shafts lit the room's contents sparingly so that the eye could never be entirely sure if shapes in the murk were of mechanism or organism; connected or separate. The sound of steam escaping in short, controlled bursts came from somewhere in the junkyard of creation. Loosestrife twisted and turned through the maze of machinery without looking. Occasionally he slowed to step over something unseen in the dark.

Somewhere, a steam whistle hooted.

At the furthest wall, an air-locked door gave way to gentle pressure. In contrast to the laboratory, the light from inside was blinding. Loosestrife scrambled beside the door, squeezing closed his tiny, bloodshot eyes. Finally, he found a pair of tinted goggles and slid the thick straps over his head.

The room was no wider than fifteen feet but seemed to extend into infinity. Hundreds of crystal cylinders lined the walls, each to its own niche, capped at either end with brass. Loosestrife slid his fingers along one of the pods. Something thrashed inside the fluid, slimy coils whipping back and forth inside the cell.

A steel table at the room's center displayed all but the organic component of a broken cell. Loosestrife prodded at it with no real goal in mind. Rather, his attention was on a long steel ladder which stood against one wall. The Professor's assistant teetered atop it, feeding the eels from a satchel. Wheldrake, engrossed in his task, took some time to realise that the Professor had entered. All the while, Loosestrife observed him.

After years of silent plotting, Loosestrife had replaced his predecessor, Dr. Ragwort, by tipping him into a vat of liquid flame, only to have his right hand destroyed by the incredible heat. He intended no such end for himself, and so he watched Wheldrake every chance he had.

Wheldrake descended the ladder. Tall, wearing a threadbare brown suit, he looked somewhat like a mongoose. Especially the eyes; golden brown from edge to edge with tiny black pupils.

Loosestrife smothered a shudder.

"Professor," said Wheldrake, and bowed slightly at the waist. His ears, resting too far up the side of his head, twitched.

"My pets are doing well," said Loosestrife.

"Certainly, Professor. The charge of each cell is registering at a steady one hundred volts. After agitation, I have measured an increase of four hundred volts," said Wheldrake. "They're going swimmingly."

The assistant's lips spread into a tight-lipped smile.

Loosestrife's face soured in return.

He left the blinding light of the battery room without a word, drawing Wheldrake into his wake. Master and assistant waited for their eyes to adjust to the greenish gloom.

"The elixir is nearly ready, Professor. Another few hours and the distillation will be complete."

"I will check it for myself," said Loosestrife.

"Of course, Professor."

Loosestrife weaved his way toward a bank of heavy, reed-shaped levers set into the wall. Gripping the first with his mechanical hand, he dropped the switch. Banks of flickering bulbs blossomed orange in a cascade above them.

"The cold glow of New Light," said Loosestrife to himself.

"Greaveburn will be the brighter for it," said Wheldrake, nodding.

"Genius of this nature, Wheldrake, isn't for the likes of Greaveburn. Or you, for that matter. Keep your limited thoughts to yourself."

Wheldrake smiled and bowed.

Professor and assistant crossed the lab. In the light, the mechanical contraptions seemed no less macabre. Now that they could be seen, the mind cried out for explanations to their uses, and that was no healthy thing to ponder. Metal-ringed cables ran between hulks of metal and glass. Steam leaked from manufactured orifices in boiling sighs. The air was damp and crisp with moisture and heat.

Ping tang gong tong. Their boots drummed as they descended the steps.

Another sound met them as they reached the lower level.

Gyyyung gyyyung gyyyung.

Loosestrife adjusted his goggles.

Shifting spectrums of colour filled the air as light refracted through a city of glass. Liquids of differing colours and consistencies decanted between the alembic apparatus. It was like standing inside the head of an insane glassblower; each canister, flask and vial twisted and bloated, depicting a different facet of his psychosis. Complicated glass corkscrews, loops and spouts connected the containers like fragile intestines. They all ended at one point.

The machine in the centre of the room captured distilled liquids like a steel goblin beneath a beer tap. Its innards churned with irritating regularity.

Gyyyung gyyyung gyyyung.

Loosestrife observed a trio of dials in the receptacle's surface, their needles slowly gliding to the right.

"Wheldrake, locate Misters Lynch and Schism. We require a subject."

2

Like an eyebrow above the Citadel's burning eye, the Palace was a yellow stone arc on the map of Greaveburn. On the inside, the Ancestral Gallery stretched for the entire length of the palace on its longest side, curving as the palace did so that a person stood at one end could never see the other. Every inch of the Gallery's walls were covered in oil paintings of differing sizes. Gilt frames as far as the eye could see. Dust coated the paintings so thickly that the Glenhaven ancestors appeared erased from history by the grey film.

Abrasia stood before her father's portrait, tucking a duster back into the sash at her waist. Nearby, a nameless ancestor sat decapitated in bronze. Abrasia took her lantern from his ear where she had hung it. In the amber glow, her complexion had the appearance of porcelain.

Her father stared out of his frame, a glint of mischief in his eye. She shared his sand coloured hair which fell to her waist in wave after wave of uncontrollable ripples. She touched her cheek, where there had once been a rash caused by his nuzzling beard.

A grumble in her stomach told her that she had missed another meal. Turning away, Abrasia clapped a hand to her neck. She massaged the muscular knot. How long had she been staring up?

As she swept along the threadbare carpet, her dress whispered like the passing of a spirit. Folds of green silk held her undeveloped frame. The dress had neither corset nor bustle as fashion demanded. It still smelled faintly of her mother at the neckline. In the lantern's glow, anyone would have mistaken Abrasia for a ghost-child.

Abrasia had held the esteem of every young lord in Greaveburn at some time or other, and often their father's at the same time. The girl's rather plain nobility could never be mistaken for unbridled beauty. Still, she was striking, well proportioned. Her slender hips made serpentine movements in her dress. There was still much growing to do, she told herself, still time for breasts and hips and all those other things to come about as she moved toward her seventeenth year.

Reaching the sweeping staircase which lead down to the lower halls, she froze.

A sound. Somewhere in the encroaching darkness at her back. Somewhere beyond the pool of lamplight that kept her safe. Sweat prickled the nape of her neck. No-one came here. No-one but her. Not unless they were waiting for her.

Knuckles paling on the staircase's balustrade, Abrasia slipped out of her ankle boots which she kept unlaced for just such an occasion.

She span around.

Searching the dark, a crease deepened between her eyebrows. Lately, that tiny wrinkle had become a permanent scar.

She could see nothing. No-one. But another noise, slight as a whisper, sent her running down the staircase, trailing emerald. She sprinted along another dark passageway, bare feet slapping the ground, before barging out into the open air.

Sunlight. Safety.

The courtyard, which had been beautiful and green, now resembled a swamp, and had begun to smell like one. The recent torrent of rain had collected on the lawn, lapping at the cloister. Tall grasses protruded from slimy water.

Abrasia grasped the railing to catch her breath but soon moved away again when she imagined something beneath the slime; slithering in its quest for her ankle. She shivered. Circling the cloister's perimeter, she stayed huddled to the wall, in the shade of the stone arches, and burst through another door.

Shadows clustered around her as she stepped into this new space. Abrasia increased the glow of her lantern, and the shadows skittered away. Natural light so rarely touched the inside of the palace.

This area hadn't been part of the original building, being added only forty years before; much before Abrasia's time, but a heartbeat in the life of Greaveburn. Her father had built it to keep his fondest advisor close. It was that ramshackle tower that Abrasia now walked toward.

Her father had ignored protests from his subjects, something he didn't take lightly, and attached a tower directly to the palace. The location of the quarry from which the palace's yellow stone had been taken was lost before the palace itself was completed. So, the Astrology Tower had been built from more ordinary materials. It stuck out from the palace's eastern tip like a thumb that had lost blood flow and was ready to drop off.

Inside the building, the joint between palace and tower was obvious. Wallpaper ended in a torn line, the carpet stopped abruptly, and everything gave way to bare, chunky stonework. Abrasia shouldered the door, eventually managing to slip through the small gap.

In the stairwell's tight spiral, she could never see further than two steps in front of or behind her. Her eyes repeatedly searched up and down.

The tower harkened back to a period of Greaveburn's history when buildings were ugly but practical. It was a way of thinking that appealed to Abrasia. Give her chunky, solid stonework over flamboyant self-indulgence any day. She hated the Citadel's façade especially, where every inch of wall was crowded with effigies of long-forgotten saints and nobles; a thousand little staring faces. It gave her the shivers.

Another heavy door swung open to reveal a small circular room at the tower's summit. Abrasia hopped over a gap in the floor; a trench which surrounded the central wooden platform and bore a sunken rail so that the Astrologer's telescope could move around the perimeter of the room by a series of cranks and pulleys that hung above the rotating chair.

Abrasia's feet didn't make a sound when she landed.

"Do come in," said the figure bent over a desk. The only thing recognisable above the semicircle of hunched shoulder was the point of a floppy cap. Abrasia listened to the scribbling and scraping of pencil and ruler, noting the occasional silence when a pair of compass' were used. "Do take a seat, I'll be with you in a moment."

Abrasia sat on a low bench at the edge of the circular platform and waited.

After ten minutes of frantic scribbling, the astronomer span on his stool. His feet dangled precariously above the floor. Abrasia wondered how he managed to hop up there.

"I've been looking forward to seeing you since last Thursday," Cluracan said.

"Really?" said Abrasia, unable to stop a smile from creeping across her face, her heart-pounding escape from the monsters of her imagination all but forgotten. "If you've known that I was coming, why didn't you make sure your work would be finished before I arrived?"

"Astronomy and divination are not exact practices, my dear. It's all well and good knowing the future but if you have no self-restraint you'll leave nothing to chance. Where is the fun in life without a little surprise?"

"I suppose you're right."

The old man gave a dusty, coffin-laugh.

"I suppose so," he said. "Now, what can I do for Lady Glenhaven today? A foretelling of her future, the divination of a handsome dark stranger in her near future perhaps?"

"Would it be true?"

"No."

"Then I'll skip it if it's all the same to you."

"As you wish my dear," said Cluracan. The girl had inherited her father's forthright attitude, it seemed. "What about a cup of tea instead?"

The old man had already turned away.

"I get the feeling that I'll get a cup whether I want one or not," said Abrasia.

A perfume of herbs and flowers rose from Cluracan's clear green tea. The cups themselves were tiny and thin as paper. Abrasia held it in both hands.

"And so what *is* the purpose of your visit?" asked Cluracan, sipping at his own steaming cup.

"Do I need a reason?" asked Abrasia. "Can't I visit simply for the love of the thing?"

"And why would a young strip of a girl, with every man in Greaveburn after her hand, want to visit a dried up old crab like me?" asked Cluracan.

She fell silent. With eyes fixed on her teacup, Abrasia thought about how to proceed.

Cluracan nodded to himself, and gave a smile that snapped shut when Abarasia looked back to him.

"I *have* come for a fortune told," she said, sipping at

her tea, and not making eye contact. "But it's not my own."

"I know. Don't look so surprised, the duster in your belt tells more than your face ever would. He'd be pleased that his picture is well cared for. But it's not a fortune I wish to tell. How many times must you ask a weary old man for the very thing that he can't give?"

"You're neither weary nor old. You're just-" a sip of her tea "-well fermented."

She could feel the laughter welling in her throat, the opposite of a lump before weeping, and tried to hold it in with all her might. Her lip quivered. Using his walking stick as an oar, Cluracan wheeled himself across the floor on his stool. Coming close to her face, he lifted her chin. He watched as the laugher reared its head in tears and was comforted at the strain in her face.

"Like," he paused, "a *fart?*"

Like a cracked water pipe, Abrasia's laughter burst, spraying the world with the healthiest of guffaws.

"Your father used to laugh like that," said Cluracan. "If you remember. He also liked fart jokes."

The girl's chuckles came to a shuddering stop. A droplet fell from her cheek and into the teacup with a *poit.*

"I remember," she said.

"My dear, the stars are creatures of the heavens. They show us our future if we wish to look, and will whisper the past if we care to listen. I'm sure, though I have yet to meet any of them, that they would not wish their gift to be used to cause grief," said Cluracan.

"The grief ended a long time ago, Cluracan. This is a search for truth."

Abrasia set her teacup gently into the valleys of green in her lap.

"I believe you already know the truth."

"Maybe so," said Abrasia. She stood and walked to the edge of the platform to stare out of the window, holding her teacup in both palms like a well-dressed beggar. "And it would serve me well if I had my suspicions confirmed. Then I could protect myself from Father's fate."

"Do you think that your father was ignorant of his situation? He was not an ignorant man," observed Cluracan, who had followed her movements by the swivel of his stool.

Abrasia span around.

"Don't you dare patronize me."

Cluracan waved a hand, wafting away Abrasia's anger like a fly.

"Knowledge isn't necessarily protection. In fact, a healthy dose of ignorance may be your salvation, my dear. Unsure of whom *not* to trust, you're forced to trust no one. Clearly a safer stance to take."

"You have a twisted view of the world," said Abrasia, who turned away from the old man with a swirl of gold and green.

"You're not the first, nor will you be the last to say it. I suppose that a man with his eye trained on the heavens must lose some contact with the terrestrial." Clasping his hands together on his misshapen knees, Cluracan nodded in solemn resignation. "But I stand firm by my advice."

"So I shouldn't trust you, either?" asked Abrasia, with a restrained smile on her lips.

"Especially not me! If you trust those closest to you, your enemies will use them against you. I neither wish to be a target nor a traitor, thank you very much."

Cluracan had dropped the hint she needed, whether purposefully or not and now Abrasia knew. She tried to hide her smile, instead continuing their banter.

"If I don't trust you, then I should ignore your advice, and that would mean trusting everyone, even the obvious threats on my life. You're most confusing, Cluracan."

He tapped his nose with a gnarled finger and smiled.

"If I weren't, where would be the mystery?"

3

Captain Steadfast stepped out of the Archduke's office, helmet tucked under his arm. He'd performed The Duty under two rulers; the late King Glenhaven and, now, Archduke Choler. His allegiance, as defined by The Duty, lay with the Royal family and so his true charge was the Lady Abrasia. But Steadfast liked his fingernails attached and his guts on the inside, and so he worked for the Archduke until Lady Abrasia ascended to the throne. If she ever made it.

Life had been easier when Steadfast was a sergeant. Captain Darrant had never strayed from Lady Abrasia's side since her father was murdered; dancing a precarious tango with the Archduke's wrath on a daily basis until Darrant's end, when Archduke Choler dealt with the ex-Captain's alleged sedition with something a little swifter than justice should allow.

There were limits, Darrant would say in the days when Steadfast was still a recruit, to what should and shouldn't be done in the service of Archduke Choler and his clan. A line not to be crossed. And while

Darrant was dusting it off like an archaeologist and pointing it out there had been no problem for Steadfast to stay on the side of Right. But Darrant was gone, and now there was no one to show the way. Since stepping into his predecessor's shoes, Captain Steadfast found himself kicking the dirt and finding the line was gone.

Two guards, Sergeant Barghest and a new Constable, stood at either side of the Archduke's doors. Steadfast stepped out from between them and turned about. He looked Barghest up and down; at the twin row of buttons that ran down the sergeant's uniform jacket. Each one strained at their holes in an effort to contain the ample stomach.

"Your buttons are a disgrace, Sergeant," he said.

"Yes sir, sorry sir."

Steadfast looked to the new boy. His uniform was crisp, the dark blue not yet faded by a thousand washes. His mother had ironed in the creases no doubt.

"Constable, at the end of your shift, please lend the Sergeant some of your brass polish."

"Urm, yes sir."

"Good lad. How are you feeling boys?"

"Fighting fit, sir," said Barghest. The new lad nodded along.

"Good," continued Steadfast. "Remember, the Archduke is your charge tonight. No one goes into that room unless I am personally with them. I don't send word by messenger, I don't send notes. Unless you see my face and hear my voice, that door stays closed."

"Yes, sir," said Barghest. The new lad stuttered a little but managed to squeeze out a "Yes, sir," as well, his salute quivering.

Satisfied that no one was stupid enough to threaten the Archduke anyway, Steadfast smoothed back his mop of dark hair and replaced his helmet before striding away. Even so, it had been a tough decision to put the recruit on high guard duty. There were a lot of the lads off sick; three had The Ague, and so weren't expected to come back at all. Steadfast was strapped for men. But he trusted Barghest, blowhard that he was, to look after the recruit if anything went wrong.

"How you holding up lad?" asked Barghest when he was sure that Steadfast was out of earshot.

"Nervous as hell, Sarge."

"That's good. Healthy even. You're guarding the ruler of all Greaveburn. It's a great honour," he said, maybe a little too loud.

"It don't feel so healthy, Sarge."

"Them butterflies let you know you're alive. Even I get 'em on occasion."

"Should it feel like they've got razorblades in their teeth?" asked the Constable, Maurice to everyone else. He struggled with his uniform, managing to make the shoulders sag even further.

"Butterflies don't have teeth, lad," corrected the Sergeant.

"Sarge?" Maurice began, and had to start again. His mouth had run dry. "Sarge, was that one of them letters the Captain was holding?"

There was a moment of silence. Maurice began to wonder if he'd actually spoken out loud or just imagined the whole thing. He was about to ask again when Barghest moved. He ducked low as if moving under an invisible wire and pressed his ear to the Archduke's door. There he stayed perfectly still.

"You alright, Sarge?" asked Maurice, who stayed at attention but cast his eyes to their furthest corners to watch his superior.

Sergeant Barghest stood up in one sweeping motion and, grabbing Maurice's shoulder, propelled him across the hallway.

"Yes it was," he said in hushed tones. "Now listen here, lad. Mind your mouth around these halls. Archduke Choler is a cautious man, he has ears everywhere and none of them have friendly mouths attached. Those letters are none of your business, nor mine. The Captain just carries them, safe as he can, and never worries about what's inside. Neither should you."

They moved back to their guard positions and nothing further was said. Maurice felt none the wiser. His butterflies fluttered.

Steadfast took the letter from his pocket and held it up to the window.

It was a simple piece of paper, folded in three. A black wax seal with no design or decoration.

It contained a name.

The Archduke wasn't one for subtle campaigns. One letter, one name, and one death somewhere in Greaveburn tonight. Steadfast turned a blind eye and kept the other shut just in case; ignoring and forgetting what he could. But he could still remember being handed the note that bore his friend and Captain's name. *Darrant*. Written by a calm, smooth hand.

Steadfast's breath shuddered as he fought back images of rain and blood.

The Citadel was one of the highest points in Greaveburn and, as he looked out of the window, Steadfast could see far over the city's rooftops.

Buildings fought for height, overlapping each other and throwing the streets below into constant darkness when the sun could no longer pass the towering architecture. Many newer buildings had been built on top of their predecessors; ancient sites amalgamated to form the foundations of another. If one were to stand next to the Temple for instance, you could see the ages of Greaveburn in the stonework like seams of rock in a geological diagram.

Steadfast picked out landmarks in his mind, desperately trying to delay delivery of the Archduke's letter. The twin domes of St. Agatha's cathedral; the sky bridge that linked the Pinnacle's towers; the vast sloping mass of the Temple, the oldest building in all of Greaveburn. The thing that always drew his eye, something that both disgusted and enthralled, was the decrepit magnificence of Greaveburn Belfry. The only building higher than the Citadel, its enormous buttresses were the crumbling stone fingers of a God clutching at the earth. Because of their size, a whole district had been built in the shadows of the Belfry's buttresses. That place wasn't easy to inhabit. The tower had a nasty habit of shedding rubble in high winds. No one climbed the Belfry and hadn't for longer than Steadfast could remember. The giant bell would toll only in the breeze.

As the sun dipped below the horizon, windows all over Greaveburn flickered to life with the soft glow of gas lamps. Looking at the city gave Steadfast no comfort tonight. Tonight his home appeared on the brink of collapse, the skyline ready to fold in on itself like the petals of a great stone rose.

His fingers rubbed at the paper in his hand, feeling the grain, trying to sense the secret it held with his fingertips.

Let this not be Abrasia's letter, he thought. *Not yet.*

He knew what he should do, and he knew what he *would* do. He would deliver the letter. That was The Duty.

He tucked it away, tugging at the hem of his uniform jacket to smooth creases that weren't there. He tested the unsheathing of his sword. He smoothed back his hair again and buffed an invisible speck from his helmet.

With nothing more to stall him, Steadfast stepped away from the twilight window.

4

The Shackles. The lowest point in Greaveburn, both metaphorically and geographically. There were no streets. Dwellings sprang from the dirt wherever there was room, and sometimes where there wasn't. Where there had once been cobbles, there was now only mud and manure. A swarm of urchins ran through the street, their bare legs mottled with dirt. The noise of their passing mingled with the screams of victims, yells of dreaming drunkards and general commotion of the Shackles' way of life. Somewhere a pig squealed.

"I don't remember ever being that age," said Schism from his place in the alleyway. "Is that bad?"

"Prob'ly not." Lynch skulked in the shadows. He was older than his companion; sparse whiskers and a pock-marked face aged him further. A battered old hat had been crammed down over his receding hair. He *hawk*ed and squirted thick saliva between a gap in his teeth.

"Do you think that had something to do with my life choices?" asked Schism.

Lynch grumbled, but replied: "Doubt it. Don't see

many other ways to grottin' go. If there was another way, we wouldn't be here."

"I'm not so sure," said Schism. "People are lazy by nature. They take the route of least resistance."

"Have you been grottin' *readin'*?" asked Lynch. He took a step away from his partner as if it were catching.

"Books get used for everything but reading around here. It spoils the good bits when you've got to scratch off the body fluids before you can see the words. Anyway, you know what I think about reading. If I want information, I get you to beat it out of someone who knows."

"Best grottin' way too."

"It's just this waiting. It gives you time to think."

"Well stop it, you're makin' me uncomfortable," said Lynch. "Why do we have to wait out here anyway? Why can't we wait *inside* the pub? I'm not a young man anymore, you know."

"If we wait inside, he might see us and leave straight away. One of us has to follow him in. Then he'll know that the other will be waiting outside. He'll be trapped."

"You sure you 'aven't been reading?"

"No, it's just natural genius."

Schism took off his bowler hat and buffed the dome with his jacket's sleeve before returning it.

The victim in question, Albert Snitch, walked along the mud lane at that very moment, constantly checking the darkness around him and seeing nothing. He opened the tavern's makeshift door. Noise and the stench of stale beer belched into the night. Taking one last look around him, he slipped inside the Bludgeoned Stoat.

Lynch stepped out of the shadows.

Professor Loosestrife tinkered in the bowels of some mechanical beast, his shirt sleeves rolled above the elbows and braces dangling by his knees. Lengths of rubber tube lay around him. His mechanical hand ducked out of the machine, dragged a tin of odd valves and springs toward him with a rattle, and then rummaged inside.

The Womb was finished, and had been since that morning, but the Elixir wasn't and now he had time to kill. There were a thousand other projects and contraptions for him to start work on but he couldn't think about anything else. So, he tinkered.

As if answering his prayers, a noise appeared on the edge of his hearing, growing closer.

Shhhhhhh-cuh Shhhhhhh-cuh Shhhhhhh-cuh

He would finally have something to take his mind off The Womb and the Elixir that was slowly trickling into glass canisters below.

Shhhhhhh-cuh Shhhhhhh-cuh

"Well hello, General," Loosestrife muttered to himself. "How nice it is to see you, you squeaking, wretched excuse for a man. How can I help such a pathetic waste of oxygen today? Oh no, it will be my pleasure. Please, don't bother to thank me."

Loosestrife snickered to himself as the sound grew closer. It was in the laboratory now.

Shhhhhhh-cuh Shhhhhhh-cuuuuuuuuh

The contraption rolled down the ramp and wound its way across the lab toward Loosestrife, its mechanical guts hidden under the wedge-shaped metal skirt. But the grinding of gears, whirr of wheels and hissing of pistons could still be heard from inside. Steam rose in a distorting cloud around General Leager, snorted through outlets in the cubicle's sides camouflaged as the nostrils of bronze stallions. The charging steeds were meant to instill the image of power and speed; instead they looked as if they were writhing in the throes of death. From the top of the cubicle protruded General Leager's head. Jowls surrounded his face in folds of meat.

"Ah, General! Welcome!" said Loosestrife.

"I have a problem Loosestrife. I'm finding it hard to breathe. Fix me." The General spoke in short bursts, dragging air into his lungs, then blustering them back out so his lips quivered.

"I am so glad that you chose me to perform this service for you, let's have a look shall we?" Loosestrife reached into the tool bag beside him and produced a long screwdriver. He placed the tip beneath the front panel in the General's life support cubicle and popped it from its housing.

"You're the only one who *can* fix it, and you know it."

"Yes, but I do forget sometimes," said the Professor, allowing a smile.

Loosestrife lifted the panel aside and placed it against a workbench. The insides of the General's cubicle whirred and undulated like mechanical intestines. In the centre of the contraption was the General's body, dried to a useless husk. A doughnut of expanding rubber surrounded what may have once been his chest, inflating and deflating sporadically.

"When I agreed to join you in the Archduke's coup, I had no intentions of ending up as a shoe box," said the General as Loosestrife reached inside with his screwdriver.

"An unfortunate occurrence, I agree. But equilibrium is maintained. You took a King's life, and I made sure that yours continues. It has a certain amusing irony. I did not expect you to be without remorse or regret. However, do I not look after you as I promised?"

"If this constitutes looking after, then yes. But *you* don't have to see the girl almost every day. The way she floats around the palace like a wraith. It weighs heavy on the dried prune of my heart, Loosestrife. Sometimes I just want to tell her--"

Loosestrife's face collapsed in on itself like a

mudslide. His wrist snapped an inch to the right and a sound like the springs in a clock giving way came from inside the General's cubicle. Leager gasped. His head tipped back, eyes rolling.

"Whoops," said Loosestrife. He took a long look at the rising purple of Leager's face before deciding to twist his wrist again. The bellows around the General's chest expanded and he drew in one great, stuttering breath. "What were you saying?"

"Damn you, Loosestrife," whispered the General, his chin now resting on the shelf beneath it.

Wheldrake appeared from a shadow, startling Loosestrife when he spoke. "Lynch and Schism are in the anteroom, Professor."

Loosestrife managed to stop himself from showing surprise. What had Wheldrake heard? Damn him and his silent feet. If this kind of behaviour continued, he'd have to make a new assistant. The Professor nodded and Wheldrake moved away.

Loosestrife slid the cubicle's panel back into place and tucked the screwdriver into his belt.

"Will you excuse me General? I have business elsewhere."

Loosestrife left General Leager to catch his breath and brood in the encroaching shadows of the lab. After a while there came a sound which slowly died away.

Shhhhhhh-cuh Shhhhhh-cuh

Lynch and Schism stood in the anteroom holding a slumped man by his arms.

"Gentlemen, what have you brought me?" asked Loosestrife, grinding his hands together like a pestle and mortar.

"Just what you ordered Professor," said Schism. "A live one this time."

"Perfect. How long does he have left? I believe that you gentlemen are by far a better judge."

"We left the knife in," said Lynch, "so that he didn't

bleed to death. A gut wound'll bleed forever before you die."

"Just remove it whenever you're ready to do what it is you're doing," said Schism.

"Perfect. Wheldrake, bring him."

The body snatchers dropped the man to the ground. Wheldrake moved forward and, despite his lithe frame, hoisted the man onto his shoulder with little effort.

"A useful man to have around that," said Schism as he watched Wheldrake walk effortlessly away.

"Yes, quite," said Loosestrife. "Now what do I owe you gentlemen?"

Schism pretended to calculate in his head. "Well, delivering a live person is technically more difficult than grave robbing--"

"Even though he *is* dead, he just don't know it yet," interrupted Lynch.

Schism shot a look at his partner before continuing: "Tracking, capture, giving him the wounds you specified, that's much more expensive than simply digging someone back up or stealing from a morgue."

"I understand that, Mr Schism. I think this will compensate for your time and effort." Loosestrife took a small pouch from his coat pocket and tossed it to Lynch. The body snatcher checked quickly inside the pouch then nodded to his associate.

"Thank you for your custom," said Schism, who turned to leave. "We'll see you soon, no doubt."

Loosestrife's plan played out like some nightmare theatre.

Albert Snitch, by name and occupation, lay on the wooden bench, knife hilt protruding from his abdomen like a map pin. His eyes flitted left and right, left and right, searching the darkness. Wheldrake stood close by, watching the man struggle to focus.

Loosestrife entered the circle of dim light and motioned to Wheldrake. They moved like marionettes dancing to some hellish choreography; their actions practiced and silent.

Wheldrake hauled on a chain hanging down out of the darkness. The Womb rose from beneath the floor, clanking and swinging in its ascent; something like a sarcophagus, something like a diving suit. Wheldrake grasped another chain and, with simian dexterity, eased The Womb onto a bench that neighboured Albert's. Light crawled over the bevelled form of the bronze Womb as if afraid to touch it.

The Professor moved around to his subject's side and tested his pulse. The man was stable but in great pain. Wheldrake twisted The Womb's locking handles, releasing the airtight seal and lifted the lid aside with ease. Loosestrife watched his assistant's feat of incredible strength with interest. He knew how much the lid weighed.

Taking hold of the knife's hilt, Loosestrife yanked. Albert Snitch yelled into the darkness, a scream that turned Wheldrake cold. Loosestrife motioned to his assistant, who dutifully lifted the subject into The Womb.

The sound of Albert softly weeping died as Wheldrake replaced the lid and locked the seal. He stalked away, disappearing in the dark, and the sound of his boots on the metal stairs marked his descent to the lower floor. When he returned, it was with a glass canister beneath each arm. The elixir sloshed inside; clear liquid with a cold blue tint. He screwed the first canister into the base of The Womb. It began to inject its contents in a steady trickle.

Loosestrife had disappeared.

Wheldrake leapt up onto the bench and gazed in at Albert Snitch through a small, reinforced window. He was awake. Albert stared out at his captor as he began to float in the strange fluid. He pleaded, but made no sound. He prayed and cursed and tried to hold his breath as the elixir overtook his face.

Wheldrake panicked. Had the Professor made a mistake? Surely the man would drown in the elixir before it could have a chance to heal him. His hand strayed to the nearest locking handle.

Loosestrife stepped out of the shadows and grabbed Wheldrake by the forearm with his artificial hand. Pain erupted in Wheldrake's hand. He crumpled to his knees, looking at his master and then back to the drowning subject, who hibernated in the fluid.

"It's called The Womb for a reason, idiot," said Loosestrife.

5

A t the city's edge, row upon row of crowded terraces made a clustered suburbia for Greaveburn's servant class. Backed and fronted by alleyways and ginnals, the houses eventually came up against the Great Wall; a dam to stop Greaveburn's swill from pouring out onto the fields beyond. Though the sky was still dark, a cockerel crowed. Abrasia tucked her hair into her coat and raised the collar. Although she was certain she wouldn't be recognised, there was no point taking any chances. On their knees, women scrubbed front steps in soiled pinafores, or hung clothing on lines that stretched across the street. Hoisted up on rudimentary pulleys, the clothing hung against the dark like dancing spectres. The sound of sloshing water and the snap of wet linen filled the street.

Abrasia turned a corner and came up against the Greaveburn wall. Leaning against the weed-sprouting masonry, she collected the ancient barrier's dust on her dress as she removed her slippers. From the satchel hung across her chest, she took a pair of old boots. Her toes slid into the soft leather like stepping into a mire, and she laced them tight. Adjusting the satchel and her coat beneath, she took her first and only glance upward. The stairway was worn in the centre by centuries of boots, but it was otherwise straight and sturdy, being built into the wall itself. Where there had once been a banister were now only rotting stumps of wood, so she stuck to the inner edge of the stairway, her hand trailing on the stonework. To stop herself feeling dizzy as she climbed, Abrasia trained her eyes on the worn steps, but it wasn't easy. This close to the Greaveburn Wall there was no sunlight so early in the day. Not until after midday would the shadows draw back completely; or when she reached the top. But with more than a mile of steady climbing ahead, she couldn't imagine the latter happening first.

As Abrasia began to sweat under her coat, she climbed past the first rooftop. Through a window she could see a young woman desperately trying to save a pair of trousers by means of needle and thread. The woman never looked up, and so missed the future monarch pass by her window.

Abrasia climbed for another hour, the stairway doubling back on itself occasionally until she reached the first landing. What had once been a guard post hunched like a tramp against the wall. As Abrasia poked her head inside, birds exploded out through the torn roof in grey fireworks. She searched the floor for a clean spot to sit amongst the white pigeon-droppings carpet, then thought better of it.

By the early light, far from the people and the smell and the crushing sense of fate, Greaveburn didn't seem so bad. Abrasia could almost forget. She could pretend that she liked to be alone; that she liked sitting in the dark and listening for faint sounds outside her window; that she liked being the kind of heiress who could leave the palace without anyone caring where she was, to climb a dangerous wall because there seemed like nothing else she could do.

Distant sounds of Greaveburn's morning drifted up

to her, snatched and stirred by the wind until they were an indecipherable soup. Abrasia closed her eyes and pretended she was listening to the sea. Maybe when she reached the top of the wall, she'd be able to see it.

Taking a biscuit from her pocket, she tried to bite it in a determined manner, and yelped when her tooth almost gave way. Placing it on a stone's edge, she hit the biscuit with the heel of her hand until it snapped, and popped a piece into her mouth to melt. It was time for more pretending. This time, it was that she liked terrible, stolen biscuits. When her mouth finally began to taste of sand, there was nothing else to do but admit defeat. Spitting the biscuit into her hand, she tossed it into the pigeon shed. Good luck to them. Wiping her hand on her skirt, she wondered how many ladies in Greaveburn spat things into their hands, and pretended that she liked being vulgar.

She looked at the next set of stairs, wriggling her toes inside the boots. A breeze tickled her face; a promise of fresh air above.

With one hand on her satchel, her other swinging like a pendulum, Abrasia found a rhythm. The steps seemed to fly under her feet, stripes of worn stone that hypnotised. Her mind wandered to nowhere in particular. There were only the steps. So when there were no more steps to be had Abrasia nearly fell forward with the effort of climbing thin air. A gust hit her in the face, blowing her hair out behind and making her rock backward. Clean air, carrying the heaviness of pollen and sun-warmed leaves.

Abrasia's eyes squinted in the light, and then widened.

The causeway at the wall's summit was wider than most Greaveburn roads; three carriages could have ridden comfortably side by side around the perimeter of the whole city. But that was in a bygone age, long before Abrasia's history books were even written. Now, grasses sprouted from between the causeway's cracked flagstones until the elevated road was a vast lawn. Flowers decorated the battlements in banks of palest blue and yellow that Abrasia could have lost herself in. But it was the trees that caught Abrasia's breath. Their roots buried deep into the stone, coiling like fossilised snakes where soldiers had once marched in their thousands. Branches spread into a woven canopy above. Swollen fruit bobbed in the breeze or decorated the ground in baubles of red and green. Far above the Gods-forsaken Greaveburn, Abrasia had found an orchard.

Her boots were the first to come off, then the coat. Part of her wanted to pick the flowers, part wanted nothing to change. Part of her wanted to sit on the grass, and part of her couldn't stay still. She plucked an apple from the ground, tested the skin with her thumb, and found it good. It cracked as her teeth bit deep. She swore she could taste fresh air and rain in the apple's flesh as if there was something holy in it.

But when she looked out over the battlement, the fruit fell from her fingers.

In every history book she'd ever read, Abrasia had searched for mention of people beyond Greaveburn. Another city. Another race. It had fed her childhood dreams. At first it was Darrant who would take her, to live like father and daughter in a new place. But he was gone, taken from her by the Archduke, and she had to dream harder, of rescuers, people who would see Greaveburn as she did; filthy with its arrogance, impotent and seething. They would take her away and the Cholers could have it; the throne and the pit of it. Abrasia would become a farmer's wife, taking his name, and the word Glenhaven would become legend.

But there was nothing. No village or town as far as her eyes could strain. Nowhere for her saviours to come from and take her to; just fields and trees and the sweeping arc of the river Greave all the way to the horizon. Just like in the books, Greaveburn was all there was; building and building until streets were foundations, roofs were floors, constantly climbing away from itself. Now that Abrasia saw it, her dream of escape crumbled completely like an ancient map in her fingers. The horizon was the world's edge and there was nothing beyond it but mist and falling.

Greaveburn stood alone on this little circle of earth, the river running around and into itself like a snake eating its tail. And Abrasia was doomed to watch the sun and stars trade places for all of eternity.

Abrasia's bottom hit the ground before she realised her knees wouldn't hold her. She buried her face into the grass, clutching at the sod as if she might fall further. Her sobs and the Wall Orchard's rustling trees spoke to each other.

6

It wasn't until Darrant tried to open his eyes that he realised they already were.

Some unknown stench filled his nostrils, seeming to sit on his chest like a succubus, making it hard to breathe. He wretched, causing a knot of pain in his side. Reflexively reaching for the source only caused agony in his right hand that spread up his arm and into his chest. He was injured. Gods only knew how badly.

The last moments of consciousness came to him as a blur of cold, pain and the soft murmur of demons. In a way he was glad that he couldn't remember. But if the torture that he *could* remember was anything to go by, he was sure that he should be dead.

A scratch in the dark, followed by a plume of light that made Darrant wince. His face was agony. Another injury. He would have to worry about scars later.

"Ah, the stranger's awake," said a voice from behind the light. "We didn't think you'd recover. You're stronger than you look."

Darrant said nothing. But at least now he knew that he was alive, if only because there were no lights in Hell. He tried to sit up and slammed his head on immovable stone. Groaning, he slid his legs to the side and dropped out of the alcove. His eyes fought to adapt to the light. One side of his face crackled with pain.

He'd been laid in the narrow recess of a sandstone catacomb. The taste of undisturbed air told him he was far underground. Up and down the roughly-hewn wall, some of the other alcoves were still occupied by yawning skulls and rat-gnawed rags.

Somewhere beneath St. Agatha's Cathedral, perhaps.

"Why don't you thank your neighbours?" said the voice. "They've been most hospitable. Never complained a bit."

Darrant turned around, prepared for anything except what he saw. A single flame sent shadows flickering along the walls of a small room; nothing more than a larger alcove cut into the rock beneath the cathedral. In the half-light he could make out dark shapes watching him, pressed against the opposite wall as if he were somehow unclean. Only an old woman stood near him.

He dwarfed her in height. Dressed in earthen rags, her hair had been a vibrant platinum, now dimmed with dirt. She tugged at a brown shawl which hung over rounded shoulders. It slid, exposing her right hand; a withered monkey paw that tucked itself up into her sleeve.

Darrant knew these people. At least, he'd heard of them, and as Captain of the Guard had even tried to catch some of them on occasion.

"You don't seem surprised," said the old woman.

"I've heard of you," said Darrant. "You're Sunken Ones. The Broken Folk."

"Both good names, although neither favourable," she replied.

"What would you prefer?" He cast his eye into the dark and back. Lord knew what sights he'd find if the light were brighter. "Victims, maybe?"

"Perhaps. But survivors would be more accurate," said the old woman.

"Survivors of what?"

"Vanity, of course." The old woman gestured to her afflicted arm. "We're what happens when people are sorted like insects and pinned in place dependent on number of legs and shape of bodies. Greaveburn's very good at it; you'll be learning that for yourself. But we're also the lucky ones." She looked beyond the lamplight and smiled. "We're still here. Despite the Guard and their Captain. You know of him?"

Darrant swallowed hard. He'd spent his professional life hunting people like this, and now they had him buried where no one would ever find him. Now he thought about it, everyone must think he was dead already. That meant no rescue.

"Why should I?"

The old woman smiled.

"No reason. Now you know who we are, who would you be?"

Darrant searched the dark around him, but still found no shapes he recognized.

"My name's Riccall. I'm a carpenter," he said.

"Well, you'll be no good as a carpenter now," said the old woman. "Now you're one of us."

She pointed with her cane.

Darrant raised his right hand and saw the bloody gap where his fingers should have been. Only an estranged thumb and little finger remained.

He stumbled against the wall as if trying to escape his own limb.

There had been a constant stench; the nearby sewers, the ancient rot of the catacombs. But one smell he couldn't identify. It came from beneath the ragged brown bandage that covered where his fingers should have been. He tugged at the bandage, releasing wafts of the sweet musk scent.

"What have you done to me?" he bellowed.

"Don't remove that!" yelled the old woman, grabbing at his arm.

Darrant tore at the salve with his good hand.

There was a movement in the shadows.

Darrant momentarily forgot his hand. The Demon he'd been waiting for lumbered out of the dark. It was man-shaped, although its hands, feet and face were much larger than they should have been. It wore an ill-fitting undertaker's suit that rode high on ankle and wrist, making the creature look even more out of proportion. The thing that drew Darrant's eye was the top hat which seemed to cling to the thing's greasy hair by sheer will. In his shock and horror, the thing caught him unawares, and grabbed both wrists. He didn't dare struggle.

The man-demon shook his head sternly.

"Thank you Chintz," said the old woman. "Try not to hurt him. He's most fragile."

"I am not fragile. Don't talk about me as if I weren't here," whispered Darrant, trying to sound bold.

"I was talking to *you,*" said the old woman "This is Chintz. You owe him your life. *Twice* now. He's the one who found you, boy. If it weren't for him the crocodiles would have had more than your fingers."

"You're all mad!" sobbed Darrant, still staring into the calm eyes of a monster. "Release me!"

The old woman passed her torch to a small man behind her, exposing the others, who had, until now, been hidden. Released from Chintz's restraint, Darrant slumped to the floor under the stares of the other Broken Folk. There were five of them, six if he counted himself.

"Yes indeed, you're one of us," continued the old woman, mostly to herself.

"He is not!" said another. It was a girl, only nine or ten years old, to judge by her slight stature. She moved forward on a pair of makeshift crutches of uneven length. Her ankles bowed outward as if under some great weight. A curvature to her spine lifted her left shoulder high. Darrant saw a flash of Abrasia in this blonde girl. Abrasia as he saw her, still a little girl, despite her sixteen years. "A loss of a finger and his face doesn't make him one of us. Look how he stares at me!"

The girl spoke like a baroness.

"I didn't mean the fingers or the face-"

Darrant shook himself. *Why do they keep talking about my face?*

"-This man had a run in with the guard. That makes him an outlaw. That makes him one of us," said the old woman. She had taken a stool and was regarding Darrant as the others were; like a specimen in a Petri dish.

"What do you think he did, Mrs Foible?" asked a husky voice from a pretty woman in the corner, pretty despite the scar that grew across her left cheek like a mould and the milky whiteness of the eye. She tugged at her hair as Darrant looked at her, pulling dark blonde tresses across her face.

"I don't know," said the old woman. "But whatever it was, it's done with now."

The man with the torch sat next to the pretty, disfigured girl. He looked entirely normal, wearing an old waistcoat and battered shirt. He was barefoot. There was no physical deformity, but a severe twitch in his neck made him clear his throat constantly.

"What if it *cfgh* was murder?" he asked, battling with the twitch. "What if it was worse? *cfgh.*"

The small girl scuttled away to hide behind Mrs Foible.

"I think that if our new friend...what was your name again?" asked Mrs Foible.

"Riccall," said Darrant, passing the test.

"Yes of course," she said. "I think that if Riccall had performed any barbarity in line with what you are thinking, Joseph, he would have been hung. I am, however, interested to know why the guards left you so unharmed."

"When I figure that out, I'll let you know," said Darrant, apparently amusing the old woman. "Although I don't count being skewered or the loss of fingers as unharmed."

"Do you have a family?" barked the disfigured girl from the furthest wall. Joseph patted her hand lightly whenever his convulsions allowed.

"No," said Riccall, forgetting to lie.

"Then you've already lost much less than the rest of us."

7

They passed through a gap in the catacomb wall where the stone had crumbled through to the neighbouring sewers. Darrant's eyes streamed with the stench of offal.

"You'll *cfgh* get used to it *cfgh*," Joseph said through his twitch.

"I'm not sure I want to. Where are we going?" asked Darrant. He was completely at the whim of these misfits. He didn't even know which direction they were going in. He couldn't find a single marker to give him a point of reference along the endless tunnels.

"We're going home," said Joseph, managing to squeeze out the sentence before exploding into more twitches.

"You don't live in the catacombs?" asked Darrant. He touched his face with the remainder of his hand. The deep gouge in his cheek glittered with pain. There were no mirrors here, and for that he was grateful. He could feel his face pulled tight by the amateur stitches; how his mouth stretched cruelly at one side.

"Of course not. That's just where we *cfgh* initiate the new arrivals. Not everyone is as quick thinking as yourself. Sometimes it takes days for the *cfgh* grieving and madness to pass. I feel I should apologise to you, Riccall, for what I *cfgh* accused you of. If Mrs Foible is right, then I was wrong, and I'm sorry."

"You were protecting your friends," said Darrant. "Most honourable."

"Oh, I don't know about that," said Joseph, probably blushing, although Darrant couldn't see through the grime on his face to tell.

Darrant looked around as they followed the river of slurry. The sewer was a slightly flattened semi-circle of row upon row of stone. He couldn't remember ever hearing about how old these sewers were. Like most of Greaveburn's eldest constructions, their origins were long lost. The group passed through larger chambers, the use for which Darrant could only speculate; smaller arched tunnels led from the main track and great lakes of stagnant sewage passed by. It was a world in itself.

He stepped over a thick carpet of mould that had grown out of the wall to drape across the walkway like a troll's beard.

"Joseph, can I ask you a favour?"

"Of course. You're one of us now, Riccall, whether you like it or not. We work and live together. I'd do anything for the others, and they for me."

Darrant followed Joseph's line of sight. He was looking at the young woman, Birgit. He nodded to himself.

"I'm sure. But it's only information I need."

"Ask away."

"Mrs Foible, she mentioned crocodiles. That can't be true can it? In the sewers?"

"Oh yes, it's true. We all came *cfgh* running when we heard the sewer cover close *cfgh*. The echo carries for miles down here. Chintz was the *cfgh* one that found you. And not a moment too soon."

"Then I owe him much already." Darrant turned to where Chintz was drawing up the rear and nodded politely. Chintz tipped his crushed hat with an enormous hand.

"He won't hold you *cfgh* to it," said Joseph.

No, but I will, thought Darrant.

"How come these beasts live under the city? I've heard some stories of course, but assumed it was a tale to keep the children from playing down here."

"It is. It also happens to *cfgh* be true," said Joseph. "They get in the same *cfgh* way that we do, those of us who were banished and come back. The *cfgh* sewers empty out into the swamps to the east of the city. It was only a matter of time *cfgh* before one of them found its way in. There's a lot of food for them here, the swamp itself being so *cfgh* polluted by the sewer. Unfortunately, they've grown much larger because of it. They're quite *cfgh* troublesome to us."

"Surely they can't grow *that* much. How big are they?"

"*Big,*" said Joseph. "If ever you meet one, make for a smaller tunnel. They're too fat and can't squeeze in. You'll be safe if you can get to one. On the other hand, steer clear and you'll never have to worry. They live where the water flows." Joseph pointed to the river that ran in the opposite direction to which they were travelling.

"Thank you, that's sound advice," Darrant said.

At the front of the procession walked Mrs Foible and the two girls. They spoke in hushed tones and Birgit looked back at Darrant from time to time, her face wrinkled into a scowl.

"Don't worry about *cfgh* Birgit, Riccall. She's still raw," said Joseph.

"She hasn't been here long?" asked Darrant.

"Oh, she's been here longer than myself. She just *cfgh* heals slowly."

"And the girl?"

"Narelle. She copies *cfgh* everything Birgit does. As surrogate big sister, I suppose. It would *cfgh* be endearing if it weren't so scary."

"A unique group of people," said Darrant.

"In more ways than one, I'm sure you'll agree. Ah, *cfgh* here we are."

Three large tunnels converged upon a single chamber. Spanning the three rivers of sewage was a platform built of so many mismatched segments that, at first, Darrant couldn't tell what he was looking at. The wood must have come from thousands of unnamable sources; it appeared to stay together by sheer force of will, or maybe by the weight of the junkyard on top of it. He could see two areas where the platform had a second storey, more like raised balconies.

"Welcome home," said Joseph, spreading his arms as if unveiling a diamond palace. "We call it Rickety Bridge. Well, I do."

Birgit held the chipped teacup at arm's length. Darrant accepted it with a nod. She stomped away. Darrant attempted to lay down his cup but couldn't find anywhere that was even enough for it to rest. Rickety Bridge was a salvage yard. The Broken Folk had collected everything of the slightest use that had floated under their home in the sewage. There were even nets on the flow side to collect more.

"You've made quite the impression there," said Mrs Foible.

"So it seems," said Darrant.

"How are you feeling now?" The old woman asked as she sipped her tea from an old bowl.

"No better. This isn't something that I'll get used to quickly."

"You may not have to," said Mrs Foible. "You have a choice."

He leant forward on his stool, reeled in like a fish.

"You can leave here any time you like," said the old woman, drawing him in further. "But the exit leads into the wilderness, not the city. That's a direction locked and barred to you from now on."

"What makes you think I want to go back?" asked Darrant, leaning away, ashamed at being so easily led.

"You have a vengeful spirit, my boy. I can see it in you

plain as the dirt on your face," she said, stepping down from her perch. She began to rummage in a pile of rubbish like a foraging badger. "You'll go back alright. No doubt about it. It's too soon now, but when you do go, you might want this."

She drew the sword out of the rubbish pile without flourish or style. It was just another item, something for the collection. Steadfast's sword. The strapping of the hilt had come loose and there were still streaks of Darrant's blood along the blade.

Darrant snatched it from her. His stricken hand flared with pain, and the blade clanged on the creaking deck. He picked it up with his other hand and began to wipe the blade with his shirt. The steel beneath was still good.

"Thought you'd want it," said Mrs Foible.

Darrant span around so sharply that Narelle shrieked. He made for the steps that led down to the sewer's walkway.

"Hold on!" called the old woman "Haven't you heard a thing I've said? You can't go back!"

Darrant stopped where the flow of slurry turned the corner and looked back.

"I know. I'll be back soon," he said.

"Where are you going?" yelled Mrs Foible.

"To get my fingers back."

Darrant disappeared around the corner.

The Broken Folk sat and stood in silence for a moment.

"Hard to control, that one," pondered Mrs Foible.

"He won't come back," said Birgit. "He'll be eaten, and good riddance."

"No he won't," said Mrs Foible, and motioned with her good hand.

Chintz was up and vaulting the wooden banister of Rickety Bridge like a hobgoblin. The trollish mute lumbered toward the echoes of Darrant's footsteps.

8

Abrasia stood in the garden beneath her own chamber window, the sun beating down and warming her skin almost uncomfortably. After the brisk winter, she was grateful for spring and the sight of the garden in bloom. She stood and admired the climbing roses in their trellis', and the smaller, ground hugging shrubs with beautiful flowers and, to her at least, no name. She'd never been a botanist by nature, preferring to look at the plants than risk a pull in her mother's dress by tending them.

The Wall Orchard seemed an odd memory now, but the feeling stayed with her. She was so small; so beyond hope or escape. And these flowers, which Abrasia had always believed to be free, were in fact trapped; growing in their blessed naivety, enjoying the protection of the garden wall and not realizing that it was also stopping them from being truly free. Abrasia envied their quiet ignorance.

Shhhhhhh-cuh Shhhhhhh-cuh

A familiar sound occurred on the edge of hearing. She ignored it. Soon, however, she couldn't help but look around.

*Shhhhhh-cuh   Shhhhhh-cuh   Shhhhhh-cuh
Shhhhhh-cuh*

In the stone arch that led to the shadowed cloister,
General Leager sat, or stood. Abrasia was never sure
which term to use. Either way, he'd rolled there and
there he was. His chariot's brass hide reflected the sun,
causing spots of light to shoot in odd directions. She
was grateful of the step which led down to the garden
and the lawn with its stepping stones. They meant that
the General couldn't come closer, not without a ramp
and much hard work from several men. He was alone.

"Hello, my dear," he said, between the draw of
internal bellows.

"You will address me as 'My Lady'," she replied.

She could run over the grass swift as a ferret and
scratch his eyes from his bloated head. But she didn't.

"Of course, I meant no insult," he said.

"Insult? You've insulted my family enough to last
lifetimes," her hands clenched at her sides, scrunching
handfuls of silk.

This was the first time she'd seen the General since
Cluracan had given his accidental hint. Although, in
her head, it had happened a hundred times and ended
a hundred bloody ways.

"I can't disagree," he said. He hung his head, as far
as it would hang. "I am contrite."

"You think that you've been sentenced fairly?"
Abrasia's face was the colour of the roses, a deep, ugly
pink that rose above her cream gown like a madman's
balloon. She'd stepped forward onto the lawn without
noticing.

"There's no element of fairness in such matters,"
said Leager, treading carefully. "However, I believe
that I live a just punishment for my deeds."

"I admit that seeing you in that box gives me
pleasure. It must be hellish living that way," she said.
She now stood only a few feet from the General, her
bare toes curling in the grass.

"It is," he mumbled.

"Never feeling another's touch again-"

"Yes."

"Being fed with a spoon like an old dog-"

"Yes," said the General.

"Having your servants wipe your chin."

The General remained silent.

"You can hear them laughing at you from the kitchen can't you? They don't even pity you, they find you pathetic. Why did your wife die, Leager? Was it out of illness? Or was it out of shame and disgust at being married to a man so cowardly that he wouldn't face the Gods when he should have? A man that clings to the tattered remnants of his life so he won't have to face judgement."

The General tried to weep, but his body would only give him dry sobs.

Abrasia watched him spasm and jerk, and wondered if her father would be proud of her for that. She certainly wasn't proud of herself. She walked back into the garden, turning her back on the General. Smelling the flowers, she waited for his sobs to die away.

"Do you have anything further to say for yourself?" she asked, not bothering to turn around. She received no answer for a long while and then only the sounds of General Leager's locomotion as it died away. She bent low to smell the climbing roses and came up weeping. Tears streaked her pale cheeks.

In the darkness of the cloister, another shadow retreated.

A draft chilled Abrasia as she wandered back to her quarters.

The hour was still early, but the light had already failed inside the palace. She swept along the hallways at speed, her eyes searching every twilight shadow as it approached. The suits of armour worried her. If someone were to have the mind, they could hide inside any of them and wait for her to pass. Every one held a weapon.

The best place to hide is in plain sight. Her father's words. And the notion was proved right when he hadn't seen his murderer hidden behind General Leager's eyes.

Abrasia spent her days wandering the palace, never missing her daily visits to the Ancestral gallery, although she never arrived at the same time. Any routine could be used against her.

Looking at the family's history made her think of her own future. Did she want her picture on those walls? Next to her father for all eternity, gathering dust until the moths and termites defaced her, erased her from Greaveburn's memory?

She finally reached the door to her room and almost rushed inside. Her hand on the doorknob, half turned, she stopped herself. An assassin could be on the other side and she had just alerted him to her presence.

Her palm began to sweat despite the cold metal of the handle.

Where the material of her dress came to a pleat in her lower back, she'd hidden a thin knife. Her years of despised sewing as a child had come in useful. She drew the stiletto from its hiding place and slipped into the darkness beyond her chamber door. If there was a next time, she would make sure that she returned before dark and lit a lamp for just such an occasion. As it was, she slid along the wall in search of a light, and listened for any telltale sounds that an intruder might make.

A curse slipped from her lips as her hip knocked against the bedside cabinet. She froze, holding her breath until it burned. The wall seemed to creep behind her, but it was only the sweat weeping down her spine.

No knife extended out of the darkness.

No hand clasped her throat.

Her trembling fingers searched the table. A long match slid from its box. Before striking one, Abrasia held it at arm's length to the side of her body. If the assassin was waiting for a light to guide his knife, he would surely miss her. Then the tables would be turned. That such a young woman should contemplate violent action toward another briefly disgusted her, but her desire for self-preservation changed her mind. It was him or her.

The match flared in her outstretched hand.

No attack came.

She dipped the match to an oil lamp at her bedside, creating a dull, wavering light. Abrasia stifled a scream as she saw the figure sat at her dressing table. It was misshapen, sunken. A spectre of some kind; a banshee.

It was the dress that the maid had cleaned for her.

Abrasia quickly checked her closet, beneath the bed, above the canopy and out on the balcony. She flopped onto the bed and started to sob in a haze of misspent adrenalin. If the Archduke never saw fit to kill her, she would die of worry.

Laid on the bed, she dozed, thinking about her meeting with General Leager that afternoon.

And that was how she awoke; still crying into her embroidered pillow. She wondered how long her guilt for torturing the crippled man would last, and wished for a slow recovery. She deserved it.

The night was only a little further along its path than when she slept, but she was wide awake. Splashing her face in the basin reduced the sting in her eyes. She sat at her dressing table, still dressed in her crumpled dress from the day before, and decided that she couldn't be alone tonight.

A flurry of activity. She washed, changed, placed her knife into the back of her midnight blue gown

(more fitting for moving stealthily), left the lamp
burning, and slipped out into the hallway. There was
one person she knew that would be up this late,
although he would call it early.

Cluracan sat behind his telescope, eye pressed to the
brass tube. He grumbled to himself in a constant wave
of mutterings. Finding something to his dislike, he
moved the telescope to a new position along its rail by
the crank beside his seat. Then he remained silent for
a while, gently adjusting the telescope's focus.
Something happened then which hadn't in a long time.
He was surprised.

Abrasia knocked lightly at the door, almost
startling the old raven from his stoop, and stepped
inside.

"By the good gods!" he said, clutching his chest.
"Are you trying to kill me?"

"If I were, you wouldn't have heard me coming,"
said Abrasia, smiling.

"My dear, whatever happened?" asked Cluracan,
noticing the puffiness of her eyes.

"I had a bad dream," she said.

"Tell me about it."

And so she did. He sat in the high chair, looking
down at her like a withered God regarding his most
beloved creation. On occasion he would ask her to
repeat herself, mostly when it came to her harsh
words.

"There seems nothing so strange about the dream.
It's simple guilt. Your head shows what you don't wish
to be shown. The meeting itself, however, now there's
something strange."

"What do you mean?" asked Abrasia, who was
crying again. She bent over on the stool, soothing her
face in the cool silk of her dress.

"The General has risked a lot by coming to you.
Maybe even the life that he so treasures. He must have

truly desired forgiveness."

"Don't say that." Abrasia buried her face in the folds of her dress.

"Why not?"

"Because I didn't give it to him." Her voice was muffled by the deep fabric.

"Do you really want to forgive him?"

"No, I hate him."

"Then, from what I can see, you have little to feel sorry for. Truer words were never spoken than those said in anger, my dear," he said. "A wise man once said that."

"Who was that?" asked Abrasia.

"*Me,* of course!" he said, and that made her chuckle.

He smiled down at her.

"Let me ask you something," he said. "Do you wish you ruled instead of the Archduke?"

"I'd have every ounce of blue blood removed from my veins if I could," she said. "I've no desire at all to rule a city. I just don't know how. Not like Father did."

Cluracan nodded "That's good, my dear, or I'd fear for your sanity. You're a good person. The task of ruling is hard on a soul such as yours; constantly trying to help the helpless, to make your subjects happy, to build a bold future out of our grimy past. It was your father's curse before you."

"But he ruled well," retorted Abrasia, drying her face on the dress' hem.

"Yes, and he never once showed you how it tormented him so. It nearly destroyed the man, from the inside out. Ruling is the perfect job for cruel men who care little for their subjects; it makes it so much easier."

"But it's harder on the people."

"Ah, and therein lies the paradox," said Cluracan. He scratched behind his ear like a flea-bitten dog for a while, and then continued. "Thinking of it in those terms, a tyranny has its uses."

Abrasia's brow crease deepened.

"Hear me out," he said. She looked like a kitten with one ear cocked, and he almost laughed at her. "A tyranny is bad for the people while being easy on the monarchy, and yet, it reminds the people how good they had it before the tyranny began. In a way, it renews their appreciation for a noble monarch of good intention. And, my dear, I believe that's where you come in."

9

Darrant was utterly disorientated. He and Chintz had followed the flow of sewage for most of the day and, by his reckoning, they should have walked in a figure of eight a hundred times over. Where the walkways split, he would look to Chintz for guidance. Chintz would simply shrug, implying in his mute manner that this way was as good as any other.

At another junction, which looked much like any other as far as Darrant was concerned, Chintz dragged him back and placed a thick finger against his lips. Peeking around the corner, Darrant could see why.

The chamber beyond was enormous. Sewage had settled in a lake. There were three barred outlets on the other side. Two were broken. It wasn't only the crocodiles that had found their way in. A hundred kinds of ivy erupted from the outlet pipes to climb the walls. In the dark vault above his head, Darrant could see that the ceiling hung with creepers and vines. Pond lilies, poisoned and distorted by the sewage, were large enough for Darrant to sprawl on. Between them, reptilian bodies protruded from the water in fringed lumps.

Chintz made a show of looking around the lake, spying each crocodile, searching. He looked something like a distorted mime, with his pale complexion and off-black clothing. Darrant looked at him, not wanting to laugh at his theatrics and cause offence, and realised that Chintz was actually no taller than himself. It was the ill-fitting suit, the cocked top hat, and overlarge limbs that gave Chintz the appearance of a dapper troll.

Chintz pointed like a hunting hound. Darrant followed the finger. A pair of scale-fringed eyes peered out of the water.

"Now how do we get him to come to us?" asked Darrant, not expecting an answer, but not expecting Chintz's reaction either.

He stalked away into the darkness, leaving Darrant alone.

"So, that's the way it is, is it?"

Darrant knew little of crocodiles and their habits. He watched the beast in its reeking bed. He would have to wake it, draw it out.

He made a decision. Marking which of the great lizards was his, he retreated into the sewer. Finding nothing that he could use, and not wanting to dip his arms into the sewage, he began to chip at the stone walls with his sword, hoping to free some of the masonry. When the front of a stone came free in his hand, he broke it into three smaller pieces on the ground.

He hesitated.

Had Chintz retreated to let him defeat the beast alone, or because he knew that Darrant would surely lose? He didn't care either way. Mrs Foible had been right, he was a vengeful man, and what he needed right now was a fight.

He threw a stone hard, missing the crocodile by an inch and making a loud plop in the water. The beast's torso rolled slightly, but it didn't move. The next stone hit it square on the head, and it bobbed below the surface for a moment. The beast had retreated, too lazy to attend to the source of its agitation and come after him. There seemed an age of silence as Darrant waited for the crocodile to resurface.

The water at Darrant's feet exploded in a writhing mass of scales and teeth.

Darrant gasped, unable to call out, and dove backward, landing hard on his behind with the beast flailing toward him.

It was huge.

The small eyes had shown nothing of its true size. It was a juggernaut with a coat of loose-fitting scales. Its back was almost black; the belly, like bleached bone. Its body bloated behind it like the furnace of a great steam machine, and water flew from its hide as it stomped toward him.

Darrant scuttled to his feet, kicking the crocodile hard beneath the jaw, making its teeth slam together with a *clomp*. He fled, closely followed by a ton of muscle and teeth.

Spotting his salvation up ahead, Darrant tried to gain some distance from his pursuer, whose jaws ground and chomped like a mincer. Sprinting until he was opposite one of the smaller tunnels, he leaped clumsily over the sewer's rivulet and scuttled inside.

The crocodile whipped around, before thrusting forward.

Darrant's feet barely escaped the fate of his fingers. The crocodile thrashed and battered the stonework of the narrow entrance, its shoulders jammed in the opening, sending masonry flying into Darrant's face. He threw an arm in front of his eyes.

The commotion eventually stopped and Darrant dared to look. The beast had gone. Not only had he disgraced himself by running like a coward, but he'd lost his quarry. No matter, he wasn't stupid enough to pursue yet. Leaning against the mouldy stonework, he let his frayed gasping reduce to a mere pant.

He couldn't tell how long he sat there, but it felt like an eon until his heart settled and he felt ready to move again. Stepping out of the tunnel, he wondered what he would tell the Broken Folk, what humorous action Chintz would use to make him feel utterly stupid.

So preoccupied in his thoughts, Darrant nearly lost his life.

The crocodile threw itself forward.

Darrant recoiled, folding himself. A rattle of steel as his sword slid away. He hit the ground, crushed beneath the beast's enormous weight. In its haste the crocodile had over-shot the mark. Darrant was crushed under the beast, ground into the walkway's flagstones as it tried to wriggle backward. He grasped at the thick limbs, trying to avoid the jaws. Dragging breath, he screamed against the pain in his hand, his side, his face.

Swinging around beneath the lizard, he found himself plunged into the sewage as the beast tried to turn in the tunnel. He ducked beneath the slop and filth, blinded by slurry, surrounded by the stench. Flailing, sure that the great lizard would be coming around for another attack, Darrant fought for the surface.

His leg brushed something solid. In complete blindness he strained for it, his hand trembling as he willed it to stretch a few more inches. Finally his fingers slid over wet metal, and he thrust blindly upwards.

The weight of the beast's attack knocked him under again.

But the final bite never came.

Spraying sewage from his nose and mouth, Darrant surfaced like a sea dragon, retching and gasping against his urge to vomit.

The crocodile flailed, its scaly chest fatally pierced

by Darrant's makeshift spear. Its tail drew deep scores in the sewer wall as it fought for its life, shards of masonry fell like hailstones. Darrant hauled himself from the sewage, his empty stomach lurching. As he tried to scurry away, the lizard's thrashing head caught him, lifted him off his hands and knees, spinning him in the air, tossing him like a sack of dirt against the sewer wall.

10

A cockerel call drifted above the racket of early-
morning Greaveburn.

Traffic moved in pulses along the city's arteries.
Carriages and pedestrians laboured in claustrophobia.
Yells of aggravation from humans and other animals
mingled with the scent of sweat and spice. Beacons in
the masses, shining guard helmets tried to deflect the
throng to a hundred destinations.

Buffeted by a wind which never dared delve to
street level, Steadfast climbed St. Agatha's Mount.
With the cathedral to his back, he watched the traffic
form clots below. The guards flapped their semaphore
flags like bluebottles trapped in treacle. Occasionally,
their whistles rose over the general din.

Sliding the letter from his jacket, Steadfast picked
at a dribble of black wax with his thumb. The letter
tugged in his hand, wanting to be free in the wind; to
escape across the vista of smoking chimneys and slate.
He teased it, loosening his grasp within a hair's
breadth of release only to snatch it closed.

He thought of crushing it, reducing it to a ball with
a black wax heart. The paper crinkled, crumpled in his

glove. A deep wrinkle in the paper began to form, and he stopped, smoothing out the crease against his jacket.

He stared into the letter's black eye. He blinked.

"You'll find it easier to read if you open it."

Steadfast jerked. The letter disappeared inside his uniform.

"Father Merrin," he said. "You scared the life out of me."

"You don't visit me anymore, Enoch," said the Priest, waddling around to Steadfast's side. Withered and wrinkled like an unwatered sapling, he was at risk of snapping in the wind. He removed his tricorn hat, and began picking lint from the red felt.

"I visit my parish church now, Father. I'm very busy most of the time."

The Priest's final wisps of hair waved in the breeze like charmed snakes. Steadfast couldn't help but stare.

"No, you don't. I've checked. And stop gawping at my bald patch."

Steadfast flicked his eyes away.

The old man continued, "They say it's the sign of a pious man. It's where the Gods lay their hands upon my head in blessing."

"That's probably why I haven't lost a single hair since birth," offered Steadfast.

"Not true, my son," said the old man. "The Gods know which men need their praises, and those who don't."

Steadfast *humph*ed. "I hear the bishop is ill. How is he?"

"He isn't ill. He's just old. A common view amongst the young, that age is an illness. He sits a lot, sleeps a lot. We run things around him mostly."

From the mount, Steadfast could see the Pinnacle's twin towers, linked by the sky bridge. Near the summit of one tower, something flashed; a flare of sunlight on metal.

Of course. He'd signed the request himself. He hadn't really read it, but he'd signed it. Two scientists from the Academe were experimenting up there. Something to do with why things fall. Steadfast shook his head. They assured him that they wouldn't be physically dropping anything on the unsuspecting populace, but using a combination of telescopes and advanced clockwork they would observe rubble that fell from the Belfry. Steadfast didn't even pretend to understand. He thought their time would be better spent stopping things falling off the Belfry at all, but the scientists had been so enthusiastic he couldn't refuse.

"Do you still sing?" asked Steadfast. "I used to enjoy your singing."

"No you didn't," said Father Merrin. "No one did. And that's why they stopped me doing it."

"I said I enjoyed it, I never said you were any good."

The old priest gave a smile that wouldn't have lookedbe sure to insti out of place on a turtle.

"Stop bothering me, I'm a busy man," the priest said, ending the conversation as suddenly as it had started. "And come visit me soon."

Steadfast watched the old man circumvent the cathedral, his battered shoes crunching the gravel, ivory sash billowing against his crimson robe. He smiled, but only briefly.

"I will," he said, knowing that he was lying, but not to whom.

11

Greaveburn is not yet ready for the genius of Loosestrife. That much is certain.

These constant triumphs are becoming most tiresome.

The first subject emerged from The Womb in just four days, fully healed and with no ill effects other than a short-term amnesia which dissipated within the hour. This may have been due to the nature of his injury, or from heavy handed treatment by the men who delivered him.

Although I am certain of continued success, I am compelled to test The Womb again on a subject of a different nature. I have informed Wheldrake of my desire to test a subject with The Ague and I expect a delivery of said subject this very night. If The Womb can also cure this most tenacious disease, I will consider myself once again in triumph, and will move on to the next project in an effort to finally challenge my intellect.

I fear that if I continue on this path of victory after victory, I will soon lose my mind. It is no wonder to me that so many people of genius become insane. It is a *true burden.*

On another matter, I believe Wheldrake to be utterly untrustworthy. His constant mockery and half-hearted subservience are becoming strained. I fear that soon I will have to return him to the lab's fourth level or destroy him. He is replaceable of course. Next time I will be sure to instill more loyalty in my assistant. Less intelligence.

For now, I am watching him.

Loosestrife set aside his pen and was replacing the inkwell lid when Wheldrake came into the office. The Professor didn't use the office much unless lecturing imbeciles or sleeping (which he did infrequently). Otherwise he remained underground. So much so that he'd had to fashion the tinted lenses he now wore over his eyes. He sat at the desk, backed by a wall-to-wall bookcase full of ledgers. Every one of them was empty. The ledger he now wrote in, with its cracked blue cover and cream pages, would return with him below where it would be stored with his others.

"The Captain is here to see you, Professor," said Wheldrake, bowing slightly.

Loosestrife simply nodded and set his ledger aside.

Steadfast came in, helmet tucked under his arm. He stepped barely inside the room as if keeping all options of escape open.

"I trust I'm not disturbing you?" asked Steadfast.

"Of course not, Captain. Anything for the law, you know that."

Steadfast had lost sight of the assistant. He glanced over his shoulder. Wheldrake stood beside the closed door, hands clasped behind his back. As Steadfast turned away, he was certain Wheldrake had winked.

"I have a letter from his lordship." Steadfast produced the letter from his belt and leant forward at the waist, placing the letter on the closest edge of the desk as if feeding a tiger. Loosestrife's smile was hungry.

The letter's black seal stared.

"Ah, the Archduke requires my services. Most irregular. Do these letters not usually go to men more suited to such deeds?" asked Loosestrife.

"Apologies, Professor," said Steadfast. "I have no idea what you mean. This is the first time I've received such a letter. The palace messengers would handle such communiqués, but I was passing this way on my rounds and volunteered."

Sweat ran under his shirt in cool trickles that made him shudder.

"Quite," said Loosestrife. His fingers made little circles on the letter, whirlpools that drew Steadfast's eyes. "How is the Archduke? I haven't been personally in his presence for quite some time now."

"Healthy," said Steadfast. Loosestrife's dark lenses regarded him for a quiet moment until he felt forced to add more. "Fit and healthy."

"Rumours are so often to be ignored, I suppose."

Steadfast's eyes narrowed.

"You have me at a loss, Professor. If there are rumours about the Archduke, I should know about them."

"Evidently not," said Loosestrife. A grin slithered over his face and was gone again almost immediately. "I've heard that the Archduke may be acting...oddly. Having his guards remain outside at all times, personally testing his food and water for toxins. Don't look so shocked, Captain. I provided him with the kit myself."

"The Archduke is a cautious man," said Steadfast. Lucky that the dark blue of his uniform was thick wool; the shirt underneath was soaked. "But not overly for a man in his position. A man of his stature, I mean."

"And what of his tendency for hiding? Behind the curtains, under his desk, in the wardrobe? Is that normal behavior? When was the last time you saw the Archduke's face, Captain?" Steadfast prayed that Loosestrife would blink. But he didn't. Dear God, the room was baking hot. The Professor waved a dismissive hand. "Feel free not to answer, of course. I respect your secrecy. I'm sure the Archduke would as well. Can't have too many tongues wagging."

Loosestrife tapped the side of his nose. Steadfast fought the urge to cringe. Behind him, Steadfast couldn't hear the assistant breathing.

"Will there be anything else, Captain?" asked Loosestrife.

"No. Thank you, Professor."

Steadfast twirled about, sure that he would catch Wheldrake behind him with a blade. The assistant had disappeared. The Captain left in a quick march, leaving Loosestrife alone with his grin.

The Professor picked up his letter opener, a silver dagger, and flicked the seal open.

"Wheldrake," he called after reading the letter twice, once for necessity and once for pleasure.

"Yes, Professor?" Wheldrake appeared from behind the door where there was surely not enough space to hold him.

"Take word to the General," said Loosestrife "I request a meeting with him."

Loosestrife thought for a while, his eyes rolled back into his head and he sucked air through his steepled fingers.

"Yes, I will meet him in the Judgement Hall tomorrow. Tell him that it regards a matter of security and to come alone."

Wheldrake bowed and left, stepping over the pool of sweat where Steadfast had been standing.

Traversing the sloping corridor to the lab, Wheldrake moved in perfect darkness, never stumbling. Entering the laboratory, he pinched the bridge of his nose between finger and thumb. Albert Snitch sat on the stool, propped against the bench at an uncomfortable angle. His eyes were bulged, jaw slackened; the cup had smashed on the floor.

Wheldrake moved over to him and, having failed to close the man's eyes, gave up and hoisted the staring corpse onto his shoulders. Yanking on the seal of a large sewage outlet, the creak echoed out into the room. Refusing to bend from his seated position, Albert Snitch slid into the opening with difficulty but Wheldrake soon had him perched on the edge. He let go, listened to the sounds of Albert bumping and sliding down the stone chute, tossed the poisoned cup down after him, and closed the lid when he heard a faint splash.

He stalked across the lab and up the ramps to the secondary entrance. This tunnel had been properly floored to allow the smooth passage of Loosestrife's only long-term patient. Loosestrife had put many of his finest inventions into use to keep General Leager alive. If nothing else, that had piqued Wheldrake's interest enough to begin prying. From the moment Leager returned from the late King Glenhaven's fatal hunting trip, dragged on a makeshift stretcher behind his men's horses, Wheldrake paid close attention. The General had been paralysed in the fall, surviving what the King hadn't. His situation had worsened on the bumpy trail back to Greaveburn, so much so that when Loosestrife got to him, he was barely breathing. His first cubicle was hastily fashioned to keep him alive, supposedly long enough for Captain Darrant to ask his questions. And that should have ended it. Leager should have died as Darrant searched the forests for the King's body. But when the Captain returned a week later with nothing to show for his efforts but a haggard appearance, Leager was looking stronger thanks to Loosestrife's constant attention.

Wheldrake climbed up through the trapdoor into a

pitch black basement, let the hatch fall closed and took the cellar stairs upward.

The house was tiny, each floor with only two rooms. Wheldrake swept aside heavy tapestries of cobweb and tried not to drag his toes through the deep carpet of dust.

Stepping outside onto the cobbles, he looked up and down the street which stretched to mist in either direction. Converting Ginnal Avenue from Greaveburn's longest alley into its longest street had been one of King Glenhaven's largest projects. It was so narrow that Wheldrake could touch both sides of the street by extending his arms. He tramped along the endless row of tiny windows and cramped doorways in the cold, his breath blowing back into his face in clouds. The poor had never been let into their new homes. Every window was curtained with clustered webs and dust, their frames peeled and rotted. The avenue's completion and King Glenhaven's death were badly timed and soon the Cholers had deferred the monarch's plan until it was forgotten. Where an alleyway intersected Ginnal Avenue, Wheldrake took it.

So soon after disposing of Albert Snitch's body, Wheldrake felt drained to his moral core. He'd say that he was a man of loose morals as it was, every man of science had to be to a certain degree, but the way that Loosestrife conducted himself was really something to behold. Dreading the arrival of The Womb's second victim and knowing that he was about to invite General Leager to a meeting from which he wouldn't return, Wheldrake thought about salvation and wondered if the Gods would accept the excuse that he was obeying orders.

He thought not.

12

Where the sewage oozed against the walkway, it made a soft lulling sound that Darrant couldn't place. Not until his sense of smell came back to him. He groaned. His body couldn't take any more battering. There was simply no room left for the bruises to go. If he carried on like this, he'd have to work out a time share system for his injuries.

Lifting his head, he was startled to see Chintz sat cross legged by his side. The piebald troll doffed his cap.

"Some help you were," said Darrant.

Chintz mimed innocence.

The steel spike, where it had pierced the light underbelly, held the crocodile in mid-air like a discarded puppet. Its front legs stuck out into space as if the reptile's last thought had been of flight. Its hindquarters and tail were still buried in sewage.

Darrant spotted his sword on the opposite walkway. Unable to imagine how he could get any more dirty or smelly, he lowered himself down into the slurry to cross and retrieve it.

"Are you going to help me carry this thing?" he

asked Chintz, who hadn't moved but now stood and stretched his elongated limbs. "I should think so."

Between them they hoisted the beast from the spike and dragged it, in fits and starts, back to Rickety Bridge.

"They've been gone an awful long time," said Joseph. It had been a day since Chintz had chased Riccall into the sewers and he couldn't hold his worry any longer.

They all sat in their respective spots; Joseph perched on a table, Mrs Foible creaked the floorboards with a rocking chair which had been fashioned from the remnants of three others. They'd carried Narelle up the short ladder to her bunk, and Birgit sat with her, stroking the girl's hair.

"If there was anything amiss, Chintz would have come back by now," said Mrs Foible.

"What if something happened to them both?" asked Joseph.

"Chintz can handle himself, and wouldn't take unnecessary risk. He'll let Riccall make his own mistakes. He might be mute, but he's not dumb."

But with that, Chintz and Darrant came around the corner with the giant lizard, its tail trailing behind them.

"Well, well," said Mrs Foible. "It looks like there's more than meets the eye to this one."

The Broken Folk stripped every last morsel of meat from the crocodile. It was enough to feed them all twice over once roasted. Joseph took what was left to dehydrate slowly into a bland grey jerky. The meat was juicy but had little taste, reminding Darrant of tough chicken. The cooked meat was strewn across a table removed of its miscellaneous contents for this special occasion. Elbows and arms crossed and nudged without care or any apparent insult, jaws chomped noisily and lips smacked. Chintz's burps echoed out into the sewer like the mating call of a giant toad, much to the amusement of Narelle, who Darrant was pleased to see eating well.

Watching the Broken Folk eat was an education. These were trained paupers. They grazed rather than gorging themselves, allowing their shrunken stomachs to expand with patience. He thought how many dinner parties he'd attended in his capacity as Captain of the Guard, and how bored he'd been at all of them. Upturned noses over tiny plates, elbows tucked firmly at their sides like battery hens ensuring no contact between the persons present despite the enormous space between. The food was over-seasoned and came in the smallest of portions. He'd often returned to his quarters in the guard house still hungry. No wonder the noblewomen were so thin and prone to fainting. The lack of nutrients and tightness of corsets would cause anyone to pass out.

He watched as Birgit and Joseph grabbed for the same meat and recoiled from each other. Joseph blushed. Darrant chuckled to himself.

"This is a fine gift for your new family," said Mrs Foible, sucking on a gigantic rib she'd been working on for some time.

"It was far from selfless," said Darrant.

"None-the-less, the fact that you brought it back rather than leaving the carcass to rot. That shows something of your mind, Riccall," she said.

"Yes, it shows that he's a man who delights in the death of other creatures and would parade his kill for all to see if it brought him glory," said Birgit through a full mouth.

"I wouldn't force you to eat it, Birgit," said Darrant. "In fact, if it causes you so much distress, let me relieve you of the sight of it." He reached over and opened his hand for the half-chewed lump of meat she was currently eating.

"And let it die for no reason at all?" she said, after a moment's hesitation. "I think not."

"Oh good," said Darrant, and turned back to Mrs Foible.

After the meal was over, with the others occasionally returning to the table for whatever scraps were left, Darrant rested, feeling that he deserved it. And his body needed it. Eventually he was left alone as the Broken Folk turned back to their sewer fishing. As he drifted in and out of fitful sleep, fractured dreams showed him images of his old life.

Darrant's nightmares were of a girl.

Abrasia sits on the throne, her feet swing above the ground like they used to when her father sat her there. Sheets of golden hair fall over her face. Darrant can't tell if she's crying.

Steadfast appears from the darkness behind her, a hand lays on her shoulder. His face twists into a crocodile's sneer.

Darrant watched the Broken Folk as they "fished" for rubbish, which they would later clean and sell back to the city as new. He wondered how many of his own things could have been recycled in this way. The old chair by his bunk, maybe. He'd bought that from a man in the Shackles for a pound. And, now he thought about it, that chair had been too clean to start with. That's what had drawn his eye to it. Had these sewer dwellers been to work on it? The fact that he may have been unknowingly subsidising the Broken Folk while also trying to capture them made him smile. He'd lived his entire life in Greaveburn and it still turned out that he understood very little of how crafty it could be.

The largest nets on the flow side of Rickety Bridge were manned by Chintz. He worked the same way that he lived; silently. Birgit and Narelle worked together, the small girl pointing out debris and Birgit retrieving them with her hooked pole. Darrant hadn't befriended either of them yet, but he enjoyed watching them work.

The others lined the sewer's banks on both sides, plucking smaller items from the slurry. Joseph was the most deft; his net never stopped moving. Mrs Foible struggled under the weight of hers.

Darrant was yet to try his hand at the fishing. He knew that the time would come soon enough. He'd need to work for his food; Mrs Foible didn't hesitate in telling him that.

He had no sense of time here, no idea of night from day, although his internal clock told him that he was probably nocturnal now. Sitting with his feet dangling above the trickle of sewage, he looked more like a bijou yokel than a banished Captain. His side still throbbed, although the oozing had stopped. Mrs Foible's pungent salve had been replaced time and again, and it still covered both the wound and his lack of fingers. He held Steadfast's sword in his lap, cleaning the blade, tightening his grip on the hilt until it hurt.

He daydreamed of the world above; dreams of light and sounds, the sweet smell of fresh air. He dreamed the face of his friend, Steadfast, and how he would run him through when he saw him next.

Darrant pushed the man out of his mind and thought of Abrasia.

He'd been the one sent into the wilds beyond Greaveburn in search of her father, and returned without him. Kneeling to the girl, he'd done his Duty; delivered the news. Her tears broke his heart. She'd clung to him, binding his arms to his body. And he hadn't dared to comfort her.

He chided himself for taking so long to stand against the Archduke, and even more for getting caught. There were still a few secret supporters of the Glenhaven house, but all of them were too clever to speak openly. And if they wouldn't speak, then they wouldn't stand with Abrasia if she needed them. The girl was alone in a crowd of cowards.

When walking the sewers, Darrant found himself

under the palace where pipes from the laundry and kitchens spewed soap and slops. He stood for hours, trying to feel Abrasia through the stone and earth, or let her feel him; let her know that she wasn't alone. If only she knew he was here. But there was no way someone who looked like him could make it so easily into the palace. Not alone, and not now. He had put the procedures in place himself. He had to have patience. Hope. But he'd lived in Greaveburn too long for either to come easily to him.

13

Hundreds of blossom trees surrounded the Common, shedding their tears onto the grass to lie in deep drifts. Abrasia swayed through the blossom in bare feet, boots dangling from her fingers. A stiff breeze tossed her hair so that she had to brush it aside. Spring had sprung early, but winter was wilting late. This was the only open area in Greaveburn, a hillock preserved to give an unencumbered view of the city; layers of stone and slate like a man-made mountain range. To the west, the ruins of the Old Wall stuck up like an elderly man's remaining teeth, marking the inner city's boundary; her part of the city, harpooned by the Citadel's spire.

She'd been in her room, sat at the window, holding a book she had yet to read when claustrophobia gripped her. The room closed in, walls pressed against her temples and caused pressure behind her eyes until she felt that she would be crushed. In her meteoric exit from her room, she collided with Captain Steadfast and they had tumbled into the hall, waking her from her panic.

He escorted her to the Common and still walked

three steps behind, looking uncomfortable in his skin, as if he would scratch it off on a rock given the chance. His uniform stood out against the blossom field like a gap in teeth.

"Captain," said Abrasia. "You needn't hold on ceremony. Walk with me."

"Yes, your Majesty," he said, and quickened his pace.

"I'm no-one's Majesty yet," she reminded him. "A simple 'my lady' will do."

He nodded.

"I know little about you, Captain. Only as a silent presence at Darrant's side. And now he's gone. He was a good man." She saw Steadfast's chest heave. "Do you believe what they say about him? Was he guilty of sedition?"

"I'm unqualified to answer, my Lady. Judgement is the job of the court. I simply act on the sentences," he said, in practiced fashion. He wouldn't meet her gaze, no matter how hard she tried. He fiddled with his cuffs.

"Of course. But don't you have an opinion? If you have to kill a man, shouldn't you at least believe in the verdict? I imagine it would be hard to kill someone without believing it necessary. Especially a friend."

As her words tore through him, Steadfast fought the urge to knead his brow.

"Opinions are dangerous things," he said.

"More so for some than others?" asked Abrasia, watching for the twitch in his face. She moved on. "Your new duties keep you busy?"

"Yes, my lady. I'm always busy."

"The Archduke has much need of you?"

Steadfast spoke without thinking: "Much less than he imagines."

Abrasia didn't answer, she simply nodded.

"Do you have a family, Captain?"

"I'm not married."

"By choice or fate?" she asked.

"Neither. The Duty comes first. It doesn't leave much time for other things."

"I wonder if I'd like to be married." She cast her eyes upward but soon returned them when the sky proved too bright. Dwelling in the dark halls of the palace for too long had taken its toll. "I don't think so."

"Men are scoundrels and betrayers, my Lady. You're better off without one."

"I take it that you're classing yourself outside the species?"

"No." Steadfast stopped dead and turned to her. "I'm like the rest. Maybe worse."

"I think not," said Abrasia. "There's something about you, Steadfast. Something that doesn't ring true. The Archduke is lucky to have a man so loyal to his Duty."

"Only a coward denies his Duty."

Abrasia smiled. She didn't have the high cheek bones or tamed hair of beautiful women, she didn't have the perfectly oval eyes. But something about the line of her chin, the wave of her hair and the slender paleness of her neck was striking to Steadfast. If the Gods saw fit to place an angel of judgement in his presence, wouldn't they make her less than perfect to better assist her infiltration?

Abrasia closed her eyes, tilted her head to one side. Her voice changed its tone, becoming gruff, but quiet.

"Loyalty is blind," she said. "Cowardice is preferable if it means that you deny your Duty for a righteous cause."

It was a passable impersonation of Darrant.

Steadfast's mouth filled with saliva as if he might vomit. He choked back the guilt but it left him nauseated.

"Are you feeling better, my Lady?"

"Yes. The open air is maybe what I needed. Maybe I should stop hiding so much."

"What is it you fear?" asked Steadfast.

Abrasia turned back to him and raised an eyebrow. Steadfast took stock of his boots.

"I dismissed my handmaiden," Abrasia sighed. "She was most upset, poor girl. Although, not a girl. She was older than I am. So far, I'm rather enjoying the freedom of cleaning and washing my own clothes. There's something humbling about it. But it's made me lonely. I've come to fear others so much that I've made myself a hermit. Maybe I shouldn't be so fearful. It may be the sunshine or the air having its effect, but maybe I should meet what comes with dignity. It's not for a Glenhaven to hide in a hole until the end arrives. My father didn't. I've become certain that he knew Leager was a traitor when they rode out that morning."

Steadfast went to speak but Abrasia raised her hand to him.

"It's alright. I think I understand. He knew the Cholers would win this time; the same way that I do. You know, I still expect him to ride back in the gate, some beast draped over the back of his horse. It'd be at night, just before the western gate closes, and he'll be glowing and laughing and smelling like musk. I think that's why he did it, and that's why Darrant never brought him back. So that every night, Archduke Choler will be waiting for him to come home too."

Steadfast realised that he was smiling, and checked over his shoulder to make sure no one else could see. When he turned back, Abrasia was watching him, shaking her head. Her eyes were lined with tears and when they started to spill onto her cheek, she let them fall.

"Poor Steadfast. I forget that you live in the same city I do. You have the same hunted look I catch in the mirror. Don't look so downtrodden. I only knew one man who didn't bend under the Citadel's eye."

"Darrant," said Steadfast. "Of course."

"It doesn't make you any less of a man. Darrant was more than a protector to me, Captain. As I suspect he was more than simply a superior to you. He was the best man I ever met. An idol, if that doesn't seem extravagant. I never saw him waver from what he thought was right and pitied anyone who was between him and his goal. He was everything I wanted Greaveburn to be and I think he made himself that way on purpose. For me."

Steadfast finally found her gaze. Abrasia's jaw had set firm. The tiny crease in her brow smoothed as if some weight were lifted. The Captain may have gasped as a pearlescent woman emerged from the girl's soft features.

"I know what Darrant would have me do," she said. "He'd take me by the shoulders and the look in his eyes would fix me rigid to the floor and everything he said afterward would be the unmistakable truth. Then he'd tell me to show my face in the light; let them remember me as a person rather than a ghost before I *am* one."

She stepped toward her Captain, hand extended.

"What do you say we step out of Choler's shadow together?"

Standing in a field of pale pink flakes, Steadfast shrank back. He reached out to her, but withdrew again. His eyes darted around. And then, sliding the glove from his calloused palm, he took his charge's hand.

14

In all of its architectural brutality, the Citadel resembled some patient war-beast. Its single eye stared outward, unblinking. The stained glass of the Citadel's main window depicted the six shards of true knowledge and shone their separate colours onto the floor of the main hall. The throne had been placed so that it sat in the centre of the inward-pointing shards.

With Archduke Legat Choler ruling only by proxy, the throne remained unused. Instead, a large balcony on the floor above was where the Archduke saw his subjects. One day every week, people could come to let the Archduke pass judgement on their petty squabbles. Who did the bucket really belong to? Whose son was the small child who had a striking resemblance to neither claimant but to the girl's portly uncle? How long did Granny have to be dead before they could dig her up for the cemetery space she held a stubborn monopoly over? But with people starting to notice the Archduke's tendency to hide inside his own robes, the courts had been cancelled. And so it was deserted at midday.

Loosestrife stood at the Judgement Hall's balustrade, gazing out through the stained glass. Distorted by the uneven pieces, Greaveburn twisted and folded as he shifted his gaze. Squinting through the yellow shard of History, he could see the roof of his own residence as a bulbous mass which seemed to push the other buildings aside.

He stood with the multifaceted colours dancing on his white jacket and ashen face until he heard the faint sound of General Leager's approach. By the Professor's guess, the time between steam jets meant that the General was labouring uphill. That would place him on the large spiral stairway which had been covered with a smooth ramp for his passage. There were several such areas in Greaveburn's more important buildings that had been converted for wheeled transit. Loosestrife had seen to it himself.

After nine minutes and seventeen seconds, Loosestrife snapped his pocket watch closed.

"You wanted to see me?" asked the General.

"Indeed. Thank you for being punctual," said Loosestrife.

"Actually, I'm early, but you're always earlier aren't you?"

"Always a step ahead of everyone else you mean."

"What did you want me for? And why make me come all the way up here? I could have come to the laboratory." Leager wheeled around to Loosestrife's right side where the Professor had left a gap.

"It has a certain appropriateness."

The General's globular features smoothed as his jaw dropped.

"Ah," he said.

He didn't weep or beg, he simply turned with a hiss and squeal of manoeuvring pistons and cogs to look out of the Citadel's window.

"Indeed," said the Professor. "What made you think that the Archduke wouldn't find out about your meeting with the girl? Are you so blinded by your stupid guilt that you allowed yourself to be seen? Lucky for you the Archduke has a strong hold on the situation, otherwise your fiasco could have caused serious hindrance. Then I'd have to do much worse than just kill you."

"For what it's worth, I didn't tell her anything. I just needed to see her, needed to see how she looked at me. When those eyes tightened, and that sweet voice came so bitter, that was my punishment." The General sniffed back a tear. "I'll carry it gladly to the grave."

"I'm so glad you see it that way," said Loosestrife. "You are a sport."

Leager's bloodshot, overcrowded eyes began to fill with thick tears.

"General, you're spoiling the moment," said Loosestrife. "Your treachery will no doubt have a profound effect on the Archduke. Having one so close to the cause betray him will only curdle his mind further. You remind me of each other. Both of you have let guilt haunt you, more literally in Legat's case. His madness worries me, Leager."

"I thought nothing worried you," the General croaked.

"Nothing in the natural world. With a little thought, nothing is beyond me. However, I am of the belief that madness is not of this world. It is fickle and illogical. One never knows what a madman will say or do. Not even me."

"Do you not think that the order to kill me came from a madman? Could you not say that?"

"Still trying to protect your worthless self?"

"If I didn't try, it would be as good as suicide."

"Ah yes, and the Gods don't smile on suicide."

Loosestrife nodded, placing his artificial hand where Leager's shoulder was a bronze shelf.

"Greaveburn hasn't had an army for over two thousand years," said General Leager. "I don't suppose

I will be missed."

"On the contrary. Now I'll have to find someone else to tinker with."

Loosestrife's features melted. The vibrant light crawled away from his soured features leaving shadows where his eyes had been.

Pock

Loosestrife's hand lashed out like the paw of a mechanical bear, punching a deep hole in the bronze cubicle's side. The cubicle, and the General inside it, shuddered once, twice, and rested. The silence, although only a second or two, lasted a lifetime.

From somewhere deep inside the mechanism leaked the sickly smell of burning rubber. Silent in his shock, Leager began to struggle to free himself of the cubicle, his head thrashing. Something finally burst in a gush of steam. Loosestrife was thrown back as Leager rocketed forward. Chunks of masonry exploded as the General smashed through the balustrade. The Citadel's window shattered. The bronze wedge and its passenger seemed to float into space.

Shards of stained glass rained across the square below. The roar could have been General Leager's final scream, it could have been the echoes of the shattered balustrade, it could have been Loosestrife's glee; it sounded like the Citadel itself was mourning the loss of its eye.

The muscles of the brass stallions seemed to bunch as they fought gravity and lost. For miles around, citizens of Greaveburn saw the wink of sunlight on metal. The scientists atop the Pinnacle swung their telescopes away from the Belfry to watch, and calculate.

Obliterated against the cobbles, an eruption of steam and screams of twisted metal echoed back and forth around the square. The sound was chased away by the first wave of people that ran toward the wreckage. Some of them looked upward, shielding their eyes, but saw no one.

In the Judgement Hall, Loosestrife dusted himself off. He whistled through his teeth to no particular tune, tossing the valve in the air just so that he could catch it again. When he got bored, he crushed it into a ball and threw it over his shoulder.

15

"Those cobbles must be like dragon scales," said Steadfast.

A company of guards had hauled away the wreckage that had once been General Leager, and street sweeps had done the rest. The only sign of the accident was Captain Steadfast in the middle of a cordoned area. He didn't stare at the crash site, but at a space a hundred yards further ahead, where a large sewer cover grinned at him.

His hand found the knot in his neck and worked it.

Whichever physician was called upon to remove the General from the machinery had his work cut out, that was for sure. At least there had been no blood; just burnt metal and some dark residue.

Steadfast now had to go and inform the Archduke of the unfortunate accident. Steadfast was certain that no one was watching the Archduke and who visited him at what time. No one cared or, just as likely, they were too afraid of Legat Choler to show an interest. So why he had to make a spectacle of seeing the Archduke baffled him. The only spies in the muttering crowd would be the Archduke's own, after all.

A Constable tried to usher onlookers away and only managed to stir them like cream. Swinging his leg over the cordon rope, Steadfast looked back to the Citadel. There was already a team of men on high pulleys removing shards of glass from the ancient frame.

"I've seen that window staring down at me every day since I was born," he said.

"As have we all, sir. Funny that I'd stopped even noticing it," said Sergeant Barghest. As he spoke, he relaxed from full attention and stepped up beside his Captain. Steadfast let him.

"And now you can't help but look," said Steadfast.

"What do you think they'll do to replace it, sir?"

"Whatever it is, it'll be a travesty. Nothing like the original, that's for sure. I'm going to inform the Archduke of what happened. This is still a crime scene, Sergeant."

"Yes sir."

Steadfast turned his back on the Citadel.

He should have gone straight to the Archduke, but he couldn't face it. Instead, he headed for the guard house. Technically, he should have stayed in the quarters provided for him on the lower floor of the palace, but the guard house was cosier and, if he needed it, there was company.

He couldn't bring himself to even think it had been an 'accident', but he would have to start an investigation into Leager's death, nonetheless. He knew that would lead to Professor Loosestrife at some point. But Steadfast knew what he would get. Nothing. Absolutely nothing. The Professor would say that there was too much damage to the cubicle for him to ascertain a definite hypothesis. He might as well write the report right now. Yes, that's what he would get. And then he'd get a smile. And then his hands would itch for days at the very thought of Loosestrife. Still, it was his duty to perform the investigation, even if every member of the hierarchy was against him. Except Lady

Abrasia. She was so different that it pained him to think of her. It seemed that all of Greaveburn was against her. Even him.

The victims of the black sealed letters were getting bolder, that was for sure. If Archduke Choler were to write Abrasia's name, would Steadfast deliver it? He had no idea. Darrant would have done the right thing. Darrant *had* done the right thing, and look what happened to him.

Steadfast strode through the guard house, dodging desks and swarming Constables. He dropped his sword and truncheon into the rack. Someone spoke his name and he ignored them. Up the stairs to his office, the door clicked closed. The bustle from outside became a murmur.

Sitting at his desk, nothing more than an old table donated by some guard's relative, he found a pile of reports high enough to bury himself in. The in-tray had begun to lean so heavily that another pile had been started next to it to save the inevitable paper-slide. The out-tray held a small potted cactus that he'd been given by Darrant on his birthday.

"It seemed to suit you," Darrant had said with a wry smile. Steadfast dabbed his finger on one of the spines, just for the sensation, and then turned to his reports.

Steadfast interfered in the City Guard very little, leaving Lieutenant Cawber to his own devices when running the police force. The palace was his jurisdiction and he wasn't eager to expand it. But no matter how hard he tried, Steadfast still had to sign the reports every week. He glanced briefly at the top one; the disappearance of an elderly man in the Shackles. He was nearly eighty years old and infected heavily with The Ague. The Guard were awaiting a ransom note.

Steadfast managed a smile. If you were after a ransom, you wouldn't kidnap someone in the Shackles;

no one there had any money. Even if you were happy to
be paid in mud and rags, why kidnap someone who
would likely die of The Ague before you got paid?
Either he needed to oversee Lieutenant Cawber a little
more and give him a few pointers, or he should feel
comforted that the criminal element had taken a turn
towards the idiotic.

16

Darrant sat with his feet tucked under him. The salve was gone from his hand, revealing purple stumps where his fingers once were. He leaned over for more of the fishing net, and winced in anticipation, but the pain in his side didn't flare. With his good hand, he dragged the net over his knee, and picked at knots with the remaining finger and thumb on the other. Beside him, Mrs. Foible was folding the portions of net already untangled.

"These damn things will drive me insane," he mumbled, handing the old woman another section. "There has to be a better way."

"You're no Fisherman. Or a Carpenter for that matter," said Mrs Foible. He ignored her so she pressed on. "I've never known a craftsman worse with his hands."

"You're insulting my profession."

"A man who arrives like you did, cast off by the guards with swords and slaying crocodiles. You're no woodsmith. If you want to lie, Riccall, that's alright. But don't give me those innocent eyes when I don't believe you." She shook her head. "What are you still doing here?"

Darrant held up the net as if the answer were obvious.

The old woman raised an eyebrow.

"The same thing as you," he said, his eyes on the net. "Just living. Carrying on."

Mrs Foible pointed to Birgit and Narelle. They sat in Narelle's bunk, their hands almost a blur as they played patty-cake. Narelle's giggles grew louder as they went faster and faster.

"That's living." She prodded Darrant's shoulder with a sharp finger. "This is...I'm not even sure. What's keeping you here? Living under the city, it'll be all you ever think about. You need to get out. To get away."

"There's someone who needs me." He held out another length of net which Mrs Foible ignored. Darrant set it down on his lap. There was no way the old woman would continue until she had her say.

"You said you don't have family."

"I don't. Not really. But there's a girl. A daughter of sorts."

"Is there no one else to look after her?"

"No."

"Well, if she's anything like you, she'll be a survivor."

"Stubborn, you mean? She is. But she's only sixteen, a little girl. When I'm ready, as soon as I'm healed, I need to go back-"

"And do what? The guards don't let people like us live twice, Riccall. *Once* is a lucky mistake. You can't do anything more for her. And being powerless will drive you mad. You're that kind of man."

"Why don't you leave, too?"

"And who would find people like you? Bring them here, nurse them healthy again?" She shook her head again. She always seemed to be doing that with Darrant. "I'm too old, Riccall. There's a place, beyond Greaveburn, but I'm past going there. This is as far as

I go and no further."

Riccall's brow folded.

"Outside Greaveburn? No there isn't."

"What do you think happens to those of us the guards exile, they just stop existing? Poof, and they're gone. Others like us have been finding each other since before my father's days and before your grandfather's. Oh, there's a place, alright."

"Where is it? How come I don't know about it?" He spun around on his bottom to face her properly.

"A carpenter, you mean?" Mrs Foible sneered at him. "Why would a lowly carpenter care?"

"Never mind," he started to turn away but Mrs Foible grabbed his shirt.

"Never mind, indeed. You're a terrible and useless liar. I know you, Riccall, don't think I don't. If you'd known about Vale in your life before, would you have sought it out? Destroyed it, maybe. Killed everyone who'd beaten Greaveburn's ruling. And then what would you have now? Maybe you didn't hear about it so that it would still be there when you were cast out yourself. Maybe it's fate, and that's where you go next."

Darrant peeled her fingers from his arm.

"I don't believe in fate," he said.

"Your problem, I think, is that Fate still believes in you."

Darrant dumped the net on the old woman's knee and stood up so that he towered over her, dusting slime from his trousers.

"Don't give me that. If you want me to leave, Mrs Foible, then say so. My welcome has been outstayed, and I'll go."

"Nothing of the sort. You can stay as long as you like, just like everyone else."

"And what about everyone else? Why are they all here if there's some wonderful place beyond the stench of shit?"

At the last word, Birgit and Narelle looked over.

Mrs Foible waved that everything was ok. Birgit scowled, but turned back to her game.

The old woman sighed. Her voice dropped to a hoarse whisper that Darrant had never heard before:

"They're scared, or they feel too safe here. Or they stay out of pity for me, and I'm too selfish to make them go. They might leave one day, maybe when I'm gone. Maybe when Narelle is older. Maybe when Joseph realises that Birgit can't love him back until she lets go of her old life. He'll convince her eventually, I think." She gave Darrant a weak smile. "They all have their reasons, Riccall, just like you."

They fell silent for a while. Mrs Foible dabbed the shawl to her eyes and Darrant chose a section of wall to stare at until it crumbled.

17

I have been most patient. The second subject emerged from The Womb more than a week after his internment. It seems that an illness requires much more time to heal than a physical wound. That would be in line with my other pathological observations. A person may continue to function with a non-mortal wound whereas an illness can immobilise completely. It is most curious how an invisible affliction can cause more harm than a visible one. I must study this further in the future.

However, I digress. The subject emerged from The Womb in full health. There appeared to be no signs of The Ague and the subject reported that a previous breathing difficulty had also been healed. The subject was so weak that Wheldrake had to lift him out of The Womb. I would suggest that this was due to the subject's advancing years rather than a side effect of The Womb and I am not concerned.

I am happy with my successes in this venture and am ready to move on to another. I have ordered that The Womb be stored away with the rest of my accomplishments.

I am at a loss as to what scientific miracle I should perform next. After extending life by both mechanical and biological means, I feel that finding an appropriate challenge has become difficult. Maybe challenging my intellect is the challenge itself.

Most intriguing.

Loosestrife closed his ledger, wiped the ink from his pen and placed it in its pot.

He tugged at his jacket, his collar.

Without his lab coat, he felt naked. The suit that he wore hadn't been out of the wardrobe in years and was utterly out of fashion. More than that, it was out of taste. Not that he cared for such things. Being cream that had dirtied to beige, he found it rather amusing that he should attend a funeral dressed in such a way.

Ignoring the mirror, he left the room.

Abrasia had found an old black gown of her mother's hidden in a box on the very top of her wardrobe. Her mother had had the simplest taste in clothes. Then again, the woman had been able to carry them well, being of a slightly more voluptuous figure. Abrasia wasn't so lucky and many of the dresses had been taken in for her slight frame. Having no time to adjust this one, Abrasia sought out a plain white sash from her drawer and began to fold the dress in on itself strategically; holding it all in place with pins, then tied the sash at her waist. When done, she marvelled at her own ingenious seamstress skills. The sash was also a fitting rebellion against the funeral dress code. She was sure to be noticed and to appear unafraid of advertising her distaste for the General.

Feeling her rebelliousness flare further, she untied her golden locks and let them frame her face. She felt most pretty when she wore it like that and she was sure that it would look far more fearsome than the plait she had previously decided on.

Perfect.

Dress uniform was sheer torture.

Steadfast was required to wear the helmet, although it pinched his temples. It had been made for another man, specifically Darrant, and the way it perched on Steadfast's head made it obvious. He also had no jacket. He would have to wear his uniform with the cummerbund and ceremonial sword belt.

No one would be looking at him anyway. No-one would tell the difference. But he did. And he felt once more the stab of stepping into another man's more capable shoes. Had he known The Duty would pose so many problems, Steadfast might have stood by his friend and superior in the Judgement Hall. Then again, with or without foresight, he still should have stood by Darrant.

Taking one last squint in the shard of mirror that he had placed carefully across the office, Steadfast gave up and left for the funeral. He had a procession to organise.

Cluracan sat on his stool, looking at the clouds.

When the trumpets rang out he gave a crow, jerking out of his daydream. Looking down from his tower, he was startled again as he beheld the most enormous black centipede which seemed to be attacking the palace. A brief second of clear thinking told him that he was a foolish old man. He reached for his telescope.

Led by the shining helmet of the Captain of the Guard, the procession left the palace, moved down the enormous stair and toward Cluracan's tower, circumventing the Citadel. A coffin floated in the ebony ribbon. Tightening the focus, he scanned the coffin and saw the wreath and colours of the Greaveburn Army, something that had been extinct since before even he could remember. The 'General' was an honorary title only, and Cluracan wondered if anyone would replace Leager when there was no heir and no necessity.

Out of curiosity, something he normally held only for the night sky, he moved along the procession, marking faces that he knew. There were few. Eventually his gaze fell on Abrasia. She walked behind the Captain, at the head of the rest of the procession, her rightful place. The white sash at her waist glowed against the black. She looked something like her father. Not in a hereditary way, but in the rise of her chin and steady forcefulness of her walk. Leading the procession as fast as she wanted to, the Captain of the Guard wisely followed her example, despite walking in front of her.

Cluracan smiled.

People found places to stand amongst the graves. The General had no friends and fewer colleagues who liked him. The remainder of his family was tiny; five black-clad people who didn't weep, but stood closest to the coffin. No-one else wept either. The multitudes assembled were either morbidly curious or using the funeral as a social gathering. An elderly priest with a bowed back and ill-fitting robes gave a speech which no-one heard for the sound of hastily shifted business cards and idle chatter.

Steadfast looked around himself. Loosestrife and his assistant stood at the foot end of the coffin. Wheldrake wore his usual moth-eaten suit and nodded slowly to Steadfast when their eyes caught. Abrasia stood to Steadfast's right, chin raised. Against the masses of black, her white sash seemed to burn like phosphorous.

The Choler family, headed by the Archduke's sister, Grinda, had managed to force their way to the front of the crowd like a bunch of wide-shouldered vultures. They chattered and squabbled, sent piercing gazes at the young heiress without shame and made complete nuisances of themselves. There was no great loss for Steadfast when General Leager passed. Had he ever actually spoken to the man? Still, a certain aspect of decorum was expected, and the plague-cloud of Cholers weren't abiding by it. He tried to hold his scowl behind a controlled blankness.

Five black coaches parked at intervals around the cemetery. None of their interiors could be seen for thick drapes that concealed the windows. The Choler arms, a blue and grey shield bisected by an adder and underwritten with the motto, 'Per patientia adveho victoria', decorated each door.

Steadfast hadn't expected the Archduke to attend. He'd either sent out four decoys to reduce the risk of being assassinated in his own coach, or he was tucked safely in his wardrobe in the Citadel; the coaches being entirely empty. Either way, the man was still deranged. Steadfast tried not to smirk and turned back to the coffin, wishing the service would end.

18

Wakes were numerous and varied in style, spreading themselves all over the city. Some of the more renowned members of society held soirees which were only different from any other because of the dress code. Drink flowed, chatter grew louder and before they knew what was happening, someone was playing the piano and no-one could quite remember why they'd gathered.

None of these wakes were as raucous and utterly unrefined as the Choler wake. The guest list was restricted to family members only, and was used primarily to make promises for visits which would never come to fruition. The parlour was piled high with Cholers, some like streaks of charcoal on pavement, others blotches of ink. There wasn't a single blonde head in the room, and everyone seemed to share the same face despite size and age. Servants moved like snakes over dark water, never giving a glass time to empty before topping up. The scent of mothballs and gin was a pungent cloud.

Arguments began to break out when the subject of succession to the Archduke arose. Since he wasn't in attendance, it was up to his sister and her daughters to stand up for their branch of the family tree.

"When Legat dies, the rule will remain in our part of the family, as defined by the bloodlines. Ours is the most pure, and therefore most qualified to rule," said Grinda; curve-backed like a striking cobra, with piercing blue eyes that looked almost supernatural. Her two daughters were no less severe in appearance.

"What about Burfield? His line is as pure as yours. I think most of us here will agree that he would be a far sturdier Archduke," piped up another Choler from somewhere within the crowd. Grinda swung herself around to find the source but couldn't. Burfield himself reclined on a chaise and sipped his champagne in between bouts of being transfixed by the rising bubbles in his glass.

"Burfield is an idiot, and would be easy to control, yes," Grinda addressed the room at large. Burfield didn't flinch. "But since he married that *actress*, his line is no longer pure. Had he taken cousin Laurna, things would be different."

Silence didn't fall, it crashed, killing all passengers and the driver. It was unheard of for a Choler to marry outside of the family, and several lawyers were employed to maintain the complex bloodlines. This was made harder by the fact that the women kept their maiden name after marriage so that the family would never die out. Abrasia Glenhaven's clan, however, married who they wished and so weren't royalty at all.

"We will *not* return to a city ruled by the descendents of butchers and builders," Grinda said. "Now, if you were to consult your own lawyers on the subject, they would tell you that Ayles is the rightful heir to her uncle. Let no more be said."

With that, the room should have remained silent until someone was brave enough to start another conversation. But, on the arm of Burfield's chaise was a Choler of a different nature. His line was weakest of all, having numerous other families intermingled in his ancestry and, because of this, his features weren't misaligned or severe. He sat straight, while still managing to look utterly comfortable. His calm confidence had people nodding along without even realizing it.

"Maybe you're forgetting about another person with rights to the throne?"

"You have none, Corwater. How did you get in here?" spat Grinda. Ayles, who stood behind her, tried to smile but scowled instead.

"With charm, my dear, something you're incapable of."

The room gasped, creating a vacuum that killed all sound. Had someone stepped between Grinda and Corwater, they would have burst into flame. The room became the eye of a storm. A few of the assembled Cholers began to suffer from headaches as the pressure rose and they had to excuse themselves. Aunt Bathory fainted.

"Of whom do you speak?" asked Grinda finally. The air rushed back into the room and birds thought it safe to twitter once again outside the latticed window.

"The girl, of course. Abrasia. It won't be long before she's of age and, if Legat should die sooner than that, probably from hiding himself so well that no one ever finds him, I have no doubt that the ascension will be brought forward. She's a most capable young woman," said Corwater, flicking aside a strand of his shoulder length hair.

"You're more of a fool than Burfield! That girl is the final pathetic specimen of a family who have marred our rise to royalty for too many centuries. She will *not* reach the throne. Did you see the way she conducted herself at the funeral? Wearing white! As if she owns the city!"

"Yes, she looked splendid," said Corwater. "And, need I remind you, she *does* own the city. She has much about her. Personally, I can't wait to see how she rules. It's been many a century since we had a ruling Queen."

"Mother, don't let him speak like that. I'm to succeed Uncle Legat, you promised," said Ayles, who whined like a child even in her best moods. Her sister, Frina, snickered behind her hand.

"Shut up," Grinda snapped at Ayles, peeling the clinging girl from her arm and turning back to Corwater. "You tire me with your pathetic attempts to rattle. The servants will see you out."

"It's quite alright, I know the way," said Corwater. The assembled Cholers parted for him as he left. He smiled to himself. To get such a rise out of Grinda Choler was an achievement. Of course, now he would have to disappear from her sight for a while. Grinda wouldn't hesitate to have Legat write one of his letters with Corwater's name on it. There were too many Cholers in the family as it was without a black sheep running around, leaping the fences.

Corwater smiled as he let himself out into the street. Rebellion was fun, but he had to quit while he was ahead.

Officially, General Leager's wake was held at the palace. The dining hall was packed with platters fit to spill, carafes of wine, and row upon row of trestle tables and high-backed chairs, but no people.

Steadfast had led the procession back to the palace, only to discover when he turned to announce their arrival, that there was no-one behind him. Only Abrasia. Rather than waste the food, although they couldn't possibly eat it all themselves, they sat at the lower end of a long table and ate in silence.

Steadfast searched the shadows, corners and balconies with shifting eyes as they ate. There seemed to be no one around; which was how he knew there probably was. His meetings with Abrasia, by sheer fate, were becoming more frequent and despite the risk of assassination, Steadfast found himself enjoying them.

When he'd convinced himself that all of the Archduke's spies would be performing reconnaissance at the other wakes, he decided to speak.

"Wearing the sash caused some raised eyebrows today," he said.

"Good good," said Abrasia, dabbing her mouth daintily.

"You should be more careful, my Lady," he said. "I understand why you feel the need to speak out, but doing so cautiously would be better for your subjects."

"No one is my subject, and won't be for a few years yet."

"And, if I may be so bold, no one ever will be if you continue on this reckless course."

"You should worry less, Captain, you'll live longer," she said, chuckling to herself, but not feeling the humour in it.

"Not around here, I won't. Around here, worrying keeps me alive."

They finished their meals with a generous helping of trifle and cream straight from the serving bowl and went their separate ways. Abrasia took a tray loaded with cold food back to her room for later. Steadfast picked a chicken leg from the end of the table and munched it on his way back to the guard house. By the time he reached it and had time to change back into a clean uniform, the Archduke's messenger was waiting for him, one outstretched hand bearing the black-sealed letter.

19

Loosestrife finished the lecture while ignoring Steadfast, who stood in the shadow of an opposing doorway. Finally, a thunder of boots from above marked the audience's exit.

Steadfast was grey from collar to hairline. He held the letter as if it had a smoking fuse. If it had been five minutes earlier, Loosestrife wouldn't have been able to describe one thing about the Captain, not his height or the colour of his hair. He was non-descript in every way. But now, kneading the lines in his forehead, the faint tremor, the dark-rimmed eyes. Now, Captain Steadfast was enthralling.

"Another letter so soon?" Loosestrife said, watching for the twitch in Steadfast's face. "The Archduke is certainly honouring me with his attention of late."

He held out his artificial hand, disguised in its glove. Steadfast stared at it as if he knew what mechanisms worked beneath.

"The letter, Captain."

Steadfast handed it over, letting go of the envelope as if it were the contract for his soul.

The auditorium had fallen silent around them.

They were alone.

"Can I do anything else for you?" asked Loosestrife.

Steadfast cleared his throat, and managed to say "No."

He reached the door before stopping.

"Yes," he said, and waited.

"Out with it Captain, I am a busy man."

"The Archduke. He wants confirmation of the letter's subject," said Steadfast.

Loosestrife sucked something from between his teeth; possibly human flesh but hopefully not.

"That's most irregular," said the Professor.

Steadfast took a chance: "The Archduke has become an irregular man."

"Indeed," Loosestrife tore open the seal, his eyes still on Steadfast.

He read the single scrawled word, and pondered for a moment. Would giving the Captain a confirmation be more delicious than toying with him? Either option was sweet in its own way. "Tell my Lordship," their eyes locked together. "She will be dealt with immediately."

Steadfast's shoulders sagged. He turned away but Loosestrife saw the man's face collapse, could taste the sweet nectar of anguish.

Steadfast managed to nod and left Loosestrife alone to look at the letter again.

Abrasia

Like a child with an empty box, Loosestrife's mind was awash with the possibilities. He toyed with the idea of using the girl as a subject for one of his experiments. He certainly would enjoy the fear in her. But the death rites of a royal heiress were long and complicated, and her body would be missed instantly. No, he would have to be more insidious, more sly.

He smiled.

Darrant stood by the ladder, stretching his hand against the pain. Above his head, the sewer cover slid aside and he looked up to see the pads of Joseph's feet take the first rung. When he was close enough, the little man handed down a sack.

"How do you do it?" asked Darrant. "How do you walk around up there without getting caught?" Something of his old self still wanted to know how the Broken Folk managed to live inside the city without him knowing it. But something newer was taking over; a sense of morbid awe and respect.

Joseph shrugged.

"I just don't talk *cfgh*," said Joseph. "I hand them a note instead. Apparently people are *cfgh* more accepting of a mute than my twitch."

"I thought it was just because you're prettier than me."

"*cfgh* There's a certain element of that in it, yes."

Darrant opened the sack as they started back to Rickety Bridge. There were two loaves and a brown paper package with greasy patches soaking through. Placed carefully on top to avoid bruising was an apple for Narelle.

"You know I won't be staying much longer," said Darrant.

"Mrs Foible *cfgh* told you about Vale. It's *cfgh* a good place, so I hear."

"I have to see it for myself."

As they walked the sewer, Darrant counted in his head. *One left, two right, right at the fork, left into the second small tunnel...*

"To know there's life after exile?" asked Joseph.

"To know that the system can be wrong," said Darrant. "I've had too much faith in it, Joseph. I need to witness Vale with my own eyes. Just like I never really believed the Broken Folk existed. And if the system can be wrong, then something can be done."

"About the girl." Joseph nodded. "The Guard were already wrong about you, Riccall. What more proof do you need?"

Darrant tried to smile but his scars wouldn't let him.

"No, they weren't wrong about me at all, and that's my point. What they said I did, I did."

"And what was that, exactly?" Joseph moved so he could catch Darrant's eye. Darrant shook his head.

"I'm struggling between trusting a system that's protected me my whole life, but knowing they plan an assault on someone I...someone who needs me. I have to get away before I can go back. I need to see Greaveburn from the outside. I hate to admit it, but Mrs Foible was right."

Joseph patted his friend's shoulder.

"Don't worry, I won't tell her."

20

Passing through the western gate of the inner city, Wheldrake remained in the shadows as best he could.

The Old Wall had once surrounded all of Greaveburn, but the city had long outgrown its stone skin until it stood only as a marker between the upper class and the peasantry. It was the smaller but older sibling of the Great Wall that ran around the entire city and was in even worse repair, a thick coating of ivy being the only thing holding it together. The bravest of houses huddled close, some leaning until they used it as a support or were built into it entirely.

Wheldrake stood in the shadow between two overlapping buildings. In the dark, a rat scuttled over his shoe. He gave it a cursory glance from one alley-dweller to another and turned back to the street. It was deserted. Only the sound of a nearby tavern's sign creaking in the breeze broke the silence. The shop across from his hiding place made his neck hairs stand on end. It was a simple stone and slate cottage with a two-storey tower at one end; a small house striving to be more than it was. Its neighbours tried to disassociate themselves by leaning away. He stood in the alley for over an hour, in which time he watched the tower's window come alight. There was movement. The light became a constant, gentle flicker. A shadow in the room seemed to waver briefly before disappearing. He wished that he could return to the Professor without the poison, pleading fear of the old woman inside.

Gathering himself, he crossed the street, still unsure of what he was going to do. He made it half way across the cobbles before the shop's door opened, revealing a dwarfed silhouette. He faltered. The silhouette said:

"Come in. You've been waiting long enough."

Wheldrake was sure that the old woman couldn't have seen him in the alley's deep shadow. He hadn't even seen her look out of the window.

Inside, shelves displayed glass jars of dried or pickled curiosities. The more expensive items were stored in locked cabinets to the furthest edges of the room.

"Now then, what is it you'll be wanting?" the old woman asked, gliding behind the counter as if on wheels. She had a warm, uncomfortable intelligence in her single eye that disturbed Wheldrake almost as much as his errand. What disturbed him more was that the other was white as porcelain, and that was the one he knew she was watching him with.

"A poison," he managed, standing with his hands behind his back, trying to stop his spine quivering like a wire under tension. "The effect mustn't be seen for a day after she- *they* have taken it. It must be painless and undetectable."

"That's a tall order. It'll be expensive," said the old woman, making a show of collecting ingredients from beneath the counter and the immense rack behind her. Her body seemed to shift under her clothes, like muscles beneath a stag's skin. Wheldrake knew where a human's muscles should be, and hers were in all the wrong places. He was suddenly glad of the swathes of black material she wore. She squinted at labels over her half-moon glasses while humming. The tune was something of a dirge. It had a drone to it that spoke of pit and stone.

Wheldrake nodded. The Professor had sent him with plenty of money.

A thud came from the boards above Wheldrake's head.

"You have other customers?" he asked, dreading the answer.

"No, no. Just me." She looked at him and smiled.

"Ah," he said, eyes rolling up to study the ceiling.

"Strange," said the old woman.

"What is?" he asked.

"I didn't have you pegged as a poisoner," she said.

It was the first time they'd met.

Wheldrake's stomach flipped.

He knew what his errand would mean, and another death on his conscience was unfavourable. Coupled with the strangeness of the shop and its owner, his mind felt as though it was beginning to buckle under the weight of his world.

"Neither did I," he muttered to himself.

The old woman worked away, grinding an ingredient in her pestle and mortar, sniffing the contents of a jar before adding them to a thick broth that started to form in the flask beside her. Wheldrake watched in silence; it took his mind from other things. Still, he kept seeing Abrasia's face, deathly pale; her eyes were cold without their lively sheen, and she was looking at him.

"Nearly there," the shopkeeper said, breaking him out of his day-mare but sounding more like an announcer on the coach to Hell.

Extracting a tiny glass vial from deep within her folds of clothing, the old woman regarded it closely;

twirled it in her fingers. Placing the vial carefully beneath the tapered outlet of a silver apparatus, she decanted a pint of congealing formula into its funnel top and screwed the lid in place.

They waited.

The thump from above came again. Wheldrake cast his eyes upward.

"Are you sure you don't have an intruder?" he asked.

The old woman moved over to the stairway and drew aside a beaded curtain.

"Not at all. In fact, I'd be grateful if you'd check upstairs for me. I wouldn't want to be left alone with an intruder in my little house." She paused. "I'm so lucky that a strong young man such as you chose tonight to visit."

Wheldrake's face went slack.

"Well, if you're sure you will be alright, I would hate to interfere."

The old woman chuckled like a strangled imp and drifted back behind the counter.

The apparatus emitted a single stream of steam although there was no heat source that Wheldrake could see. It whistled like a kettle for a moment, the lid rattling. A single droplet of fluid ran down the apparatus' outlet, paused for a moment, then fell into the vial as if travelling through syrup. A faint pulse of light from inside the vial could have been a trick of the eye. Wheldrake knew it wasn't.

The nape of his neck felt uncomfortable and tight as the old woman placed the vial on her counter like an item of damning evidence. He looked at it, but didn't move.

"I apologise," he said. "I believe that I've misled you. I will, of course, pay you for that vial, but you can keep it. Could you distil something else?"

"Oh?" asked the old woman, feigning surprise. Badly.

"Something....less fatal?"

"*Less* fatal?"

"Yes," said Wheldrake, a plan forming in his mind. He damned himself for not thinking of it before. Now he was contemplating the future of his immortal soul, ideas were forming. "Something to cause deep sleep perhaps? But it would appear like death."

The old woman held out the small vial.

"There you go," she said. "A fine choice."

"As I said, you can keep the vial and you'll still be paid. I'm prepared to return for the other item if necessary."

"I asked you what you wanted," said the old woman, still holding the vial out with a perfectly steady hand as if it were a fixed point; a handhold in the universe. "And you lied to me. *This* is what you wanted."

Wheldrake nodded, unsurprised by the shopkeeper's sinister foresight.

"Thank you," he said and reached out to pluck the vial from her fingers.

It wouldn't move.

The old woman's forefinger and thumb were stronger than his entire body. He knew that no number of men would be able to wrestle that vial from her if she didn't wish it. He pinched the top of the bottle lightly, feeling an uncomfortable crawling seep through the bones of his hand and into his arm. He held on, unflinching, repulsed as the old woman spoke.

"This single drop, with food or drink," she said. "The sleep is total and everlasting. The girl will remain in slumber, but alive."

Wheldrake nodded, only so that the sensation of squirming ivy in his veins would stop. He placed a small bag on the counter, its contents clinking together. The old woman released the vial and Wheldrake nearly fell backward without realising that he'd been straining.

He nodded politely and almost dived out of the door.

As it closed behind him, he heard a sound that he couldn't place, nor ever wished to. Something like squirming, perhaps, wet and thick. He shuddered, trying to put it well out of his mind as he strode down the street. There was much to do tonight if Abrasia was to be saved.

21

Like a dog, ears low and tail between its legs, the Wickless Candle tavern sulked in the misty maze of the Shackles. Its name came from an old thief's tale. A mystical candle, they said, which bestowed on its owner the ability to see without light, a great gift to the sticky-handed. The patrons, many of whom belonged to the thieving fraternity, believed that the candle was buried somewhere beneath the pub but no one dared cross Norbic, the innkeeper. There were as many stories about him as the candle itself.

The tavern's ceiling seemed to exert a force on the men who filled the small tables, crushing them down over their pint glasses. No-one looked anywhere other than the tabletops.

"I won't take orders from a grottin' whelp."

Lynch slammed his fist into the table. His hat, which had been resting on the surface, shot into the air. Everyone in the room heard the outburst; no-one registered it. It was an important survival technique to not hear what men like Lynch said, no matter how loudly they spoke. "If he wants me to do a job like this, he can tell me himself."

"When a man asks you to perform a task like this, do you not think that he's busy already?" said Wheldrake.

Lynch puffed out his chest, posturing and grunting like a gorilla.

Wheldrake leaned forward to increase the pressure.

"Can you do it, or can't you?"

"I'll have to talk to Schism," Lynch said through a cloud of ale stench. He picked up his drink, a pint of watery rust, and gulped it down.

"Then talk quickly. The Professor's an impatient man."

"We'll want payin' in advance," said Lynch. Schism had taught him to say this whenever a job seemed dangerous.

"You'll be well compensated," said Wheldrake.

Wheldrake stood and left without another word. There was much more to do tonight and he was aware of the sun already tickling the horizon's belly.

Loosestrife's legs stuck out from beneath a swollen mass of machinery, tools arrayed at his feet. The flash of a welder lit his reclining body in bursts. As Wheldrake approached, he slid out on a wheeled board, his tinted goggles in place.

"Where have you been?" He didn't boom or shout, and somehow that was worse. Loosestrife's words came out of him like a corpse's sigh, full of rot and dust. Although there was no natural light in the lab, he could tell that most of the new day had passed by the glow of the grates high above.

"The poison took a long time to distil. It's most potent," answered Wheldrake, forgetting to say "Sir". By the time he noticed, it was too late. Adding the word now would make it sound sarcastic.

"Where is it?"

Wheldrake produced the vial and held it up, wishing that he could cling to it as the old woman had.

If he was to save his soul, and the girl, he'd have to administer the drug himself. Loosestrife plucked the vial from his fingers and raised it to his goggle lens.

"So small," he said.

"Many dangerous things are," said Wheldrake. He was tired and needed to mind his tongue.

"Indeed," said the Professor. "You'll make the necessary arrangements."

"Consider them arranged, Professor."

Wheldrake moved through to the eel room. With the airlock door closed behind him, he relaxed a little. The broken cell still lay on the central platform. He prodded at it, fitting pieces here and there but with no real enthusiasm. After a while he stopped altogether. Spreading his hands out on the workbench, he counted off what he would need. Everything seemed in place but one. He needed only an hour free of Professor Loosestrife to complete his plan. What would bring the mad man from his hole? It would have to be good, or bad, depending on the perspective.

Wheldrake ached everywhere north of his neck. He felt as if his nose put pressure on his eyes, his eyes put pressure on his brain. He was certain that haste would be his downfall. Still, the time was undeniably now. He'd wait for night and pray Abrasia retired early.

22

It was going to be a long night.

Having left the night guard at the Archduke's door, Steadfast had feigned illness and told them not to contact him unless in an absolute emergency. He hoped there was no such emergency because he wasn't where he should be. Tucked in the space behind a suit of armour, he kept his eye on Abrasia's bedroom door. Being there could be fatal for him. Not being there would mean certain death for the girl. He tried to breathe evenly and failed.

Mice scuttled at the furthest end of the corridor and, in the darkness, Steadfast tensed. Every nerve teetered above an abyss. Straining his eyes in the dark had produced a potent headache; he moved his stare from Abrasia's door to rest them. He willed the night to end quickly even though the girl had retired only two hours ago. He had to relax. Dying of a heart attack outside his charge's room wasn't an option. He could die tomorrow, if need be.

Having already scouted the garden below the heiress' window, he was sure that someone could still gain entry that way. But his only options were to trust another person to stand guard below or to remain *inside* the room with the girl. Both out of the question. He ran over scenarios in his head; where the assassin would come from, what method of destruction they planned for Abrasia. He had a thousand fears but didn't know which would be the right one.

Wheldrake wrung his hands to stop the shaking.

Not with Albert Snitch, not with the old man, not with the other victims of Loosestrife's diabolical experimentation had he felt so nervous. Now, he felt it. Maybe he knew those lives were already lost; there was nothing he could do. But Abrasia's life was entirely his to save.

Huddled against the wall of the palace's upper corridor, Wheldrake's resolve was mud-sliding. The small glass vial tucked into his suit jacket pressed against his ribs like a knife blade applied for painful encouragement.

He had to move.

He had to move now or turn back.

Something shifted past the corridor's furthest window.

A shadow; the assassin.

Steadfast cursed his heart and the blood that rushed through his ears. He needed all his senses to track the assassin in the dark, and he'd already lost one to the overpowering thunder of his own pulse. If he was to survive an encounter against a villain bred to deal death, he'd have to be better than he thought he was. Steadfast felt familiar cowardice creeping in.

He was about to die.

No one else had to die.

If Wheldrake could save Abrasia, then surely his soul would be secure. He didn't have to lift a tyranny, only save the girl that slumbered somewhere along this midnight corridor.

Another movement.

A careless scuffle of feet.

Steadfast's spine throbbed with tension. The assassin was human then, and as prone to mistakes as he was. There was a chance. Whatever edge he could get, he would have to take. With no armour to hinder him, the blade could be all he needed. Of course, he could be certain that the assassin was likewise armed.

Dammit.

Wheldrake was almost sent sprawling by the ill-fitting carpet. That was his penance for slinking along the wall rather than being bold. He steadied himself on the wall, grateful that Abrasia didn't have guards outside her room. If there had been, that would have been the end of him.

He crept on.

The doorway appeared as a lighter shadow in the gloom.

The assassin emerged from a shadow ten feet closer than Steadfast expected. After the stumble, he'd moved almost silently. Steadfast debated whether to shift his weight for a pounce, and thought better of it. He waited as the silhouette stalked across the hallway, passing just a few feet away.

Wheldrake would have to be swift and silent. The girl had to take the tonic without waking up. If she caught him, no explaining would get her to drink from the vial. And he didn't know if he had the spine to force it on her.

The fate of an innocent; the fate of his own immortal soul. Those were the stakes.

The assassin hung his head briefly, no doubt listening for signs of movement within, and then span around to face the door.

Steadfast made his move. Darting across the hall, he caught the stranger about the throat with his forearm and pulled backward.

The assassin thrashed. He was taller, stronger. Steadfast strained to hold on.

Out of the darkness, an attacker.

Wheldrake felt the knife blade at his back, a thick arm wrapped around his throat. There would be blood tonight after all. Loosestrife hadn't trusted Wheldrake to finish Abrasia and had sent another to kill them both. The questionable fate of Wheldrake's soul would be answered sooner than he thought, swiftly followed by the Glenhaven heiress.

With a burst of strength, Wheldrake threw the combatant over his shoulder.

The carpet cushioned Steadfast's crumpled body, but he didn't have time to draw breath before the assassin's weight bore down on him. Steadfast flung his head to the side as the fiend smashed its hand into the floor with a thud on the carpet. There was no exclamation of pain, nor had there been one of surprise when Steadfast had attacked.

What kind of creature was he battling?

Thick hands pried at the vices Wheldrake held around the assailant's throat. The attacker was large, yes, but his stubby fingers wouldn't save him. Wheldrake smelled the death-sweat as the attacker tried to save his own life; could taste the mortal panic as if biting on copper.

As the man's struggles began to falter, Wheldrake caught sight of familiar features in the gloom.

"*Steadfast?*" whispered the assassin.

He didn't know the voice.

A face descended out of the darkness and Steadfast tried to scream. Bestial features pressed close to his own. The severely sloping forehead and bristling hair reminded Steadfast of a stoat. Only one man had eyes like that.

"What are you doing here, Captain?" whispered Wheldrake, still pressing heavy on his chest. Despite his long body, Wheldrake was extremely heavy.

"Capturing you," Steadfast rasped.

"You're not doing very well," whispered Wheldrake.

Steadfast caught his whimper before it escaped.

"Don't try to stop me, Captain. What I'm about to do is for the best. You must trust me."

"It's hard to trust a man with his hands around your throat."

Steadfast wasn't even sure that 'man' was the right description anymore. Of course he'd seen Wheldrake, often from a distance, and had noted his obscure looks, but never had he suspected that the man was quite this peculiar.

"Of course, I apologise."

Steadfast found himself upright in an instant. Although on his feet, he wavered as if recovering from a fever.

"You're a curious man, Captain. I didn't imagine that you'd attempt to protect the Lady Abrasia."

"And why's that?" asked Steadfast, actually hurt by the statement.

"I thought you were a coward," said Wheldrake, exposing a mouthful of tiny sharp teeth. "I see that I had you wrong."

"Maybe not," Steadfast mumbled. "But that's not an issue now. Why am I talking with the very person that I should've run through as soon as seeing him?"

"Yes, it's most unexpected," said Wheldrake. "Is the Lady Abrasia in her room?"

"Yes."

"Does she sleep until morning?"

"Sometimes, yes. She has bad dreams."

"Then I think we have some time. Let's talk."

Wheldrake lead Steadfast by the forelock. They both retreated around the corner, skirting the torn carpet one after the other. Beside a small window, both were washed pale by moonlight.

"Why is it that we're both here, Captain? I know *why* we're here, but why are we *here?*" said Wheldrake. "I think it might be fate."

Steadfast stayed silent.

"In my pocket is a drug which will save the life of the young Lady. She'll sleep deep and long, and she won't wake. It will have the appearance of death."

"Say I believe you, what good will that do?"

"She'll be removed to the house of rest and pronounced dead by even the most expert physicians-"

"This is ridiculous," interrupted Steadfast. "Your plan has holes that the Moon could pass through. She'd be buried alive."

He turned to look over his shoulder in case he was being distracted, only to be attacked or allow an attack on Abrasia. This conversation was making him twitchy.

"I haven't planned well," said Wheldrake, nodding. "With little time and much pressure to deliver a dead heiress, I've had to whitewash some fine points. Here's what I have: She will be laid out for anyone who wishes to pay their respects the day after tomorrow. That night, the night that she would be placed into her coffin for burial, I have two men ready to steal her away and bring her to me. I can't tell you the details after that, it's complex and I don't think you'd really want to know. But she'll be safe."

"Are your men invincible?" asked Steadfast.

"Of course not. But they're dastardly, and well-practiced."

"They won't succeed no matter their cunning. The honour guard for a deceased member of the Glenhaven house is six men strong and stays with the coffin at all times. No one will be admitted until the mortician the next morning. Anyone caught breaking their way in will be killed on sight. No questions."

Wheldrake's face fell. Lynch and Schism weren't men who could pass easily for anyone but themselves. It would be impossible for them to trick their way inside, and even harder to trick their way back out with a body they hadn't arrived with.

"It seems fate *is* on our side," said Steadfast.

Wheldrake cocked his head sharply to the side: "How so?"

"Gods only know why I'm doing this, but I'll perform the honour guard myself, and send the rest home." Steadfast recoiled as Wheldrake grabbed his uniform.

"You can make sure of it?" hissed Wheldrake.

"It is my Duty," said Steadfast. "And for once, I can be proud of it."

Wheldrake ignored the comment.

"Then you'll admit my men?" he said.

Steadfast shrugged in the dark.

"I suppose you'll have to trust me."

23

The news travelled like a plague, spreading from person to person through open windows and on doorsteps until whole neighbourhoods were infected; markets and churches became plague pits of gossip.

Captain Steadfast had found Lady Abrasia dead in her bed after she failed to meet him early that morning. The physician was contacted immediately, the eminent Dr. Falstrop, who confirmed the diagnosis. The young girl had died mysteriously in her sleep.

By eight o'clock, Archduke Choler was informed.

By nine, most of the aristocracy knew.

By nine-thirty, Grinda Choler and her three daughters were drinking champagne in the study.

By eleven, Greaveburn had begun to mourn the loss of the last scion of the Glenhaven house. It was seen as an omen of ill will that such a vital young woman had been taken as she slept and many cursed their Gods, fates and demons.

Greaveburn was stuck with the Cholers.

Two weeping handmaids laid out the young woman, overseen by a crone. Abrasia was removed from her bed and escorted by armed guard to the house of rest; a long, low sandstone building. Taken through the front doors, an honour reserved for royalty, Abrasia was laid on her final bed; a cushioned stone pedestal. She was kept from the public for the day to allow her spirit to leave of its own free will in peace and silence.

Steadfast wept openly throughout and demanded that he begin the honour guard immediately, and alone. Once alone, he whispered assurances and apologies to Abrasia's tranquil form for not seeking her consent. Wheldrake had pointed out that she would likely refuse such an undignified solution to her predicament, and they'd agreed not to consult her for her own sake. Wheldrake had done the final deed, administering the drug into the girl's mouth as she slept, her dainty hand laid softly beside a golden ripple of hair. Steadfast had chosen to stay outside, unable to trust himself when it came to the final moment.

The handmaids had dressed her in the finest white silk gown they could find, a spring-flower green sash twined her waist in a plait. They'd done a good job, thought Steadfast; the public who came to see her would be proud.

And they came.

The next morning the doors were thrown open and scores upon scores of Greaveburners were already there, the queue extended through the cramped streets for miles. Thousands waited patiently to whisper some final word to the last Glenhaven. Even street merchants, wandering through the crowds with their wares, lowered their voices in respect.

Legends were sparked in a day. Abrasia's plain looks became serene beauty. Some said that she kept her lively colour; the sign of a life taken too early.

The city rode a wave of emotion that crested in anguish and rolled back, leaving only the wet sand of despair.

And whispers began, putting blame on the Cholers.

24

The last few stragglers paid their respects by lamplight and returned to whatever hovel they called home. Steadfast followed the ushers as they moved Abrasia from her pedestal, taking her through to the rear room where the honour guard would begin in earnest.

Abrasia lay in her coffin, surrounded by white ash wood and lilac silk like the stamen of an albino flower. Delicate helixes of smoke rose from the incense.

Steadfast had no idea when the "delivery men" would come for Abrasia. He just had to wait. He spoke to Abrasia, still unsure whether she could hear him or not. He told her again what they planned to do, at least the part he knew.

The candles melted until droplets of hot wax formed pools on the tabletop. Steadfast sat and watched them burn.

Two sharp raps at the rear door.

With a delay to gather himself, Steadfast wet his lips, and answered.

Beyond the threshold, the duo stood like

barbarians. The older looked at Steadfast like he would quite happily eat him if he felt peckish; the younger, sharper man appeared deviously amused.

"I believe you have a package for us to collect," said Schism and raised his hand when Steadfast moved to complain. "Take no offence friend, it's a term of business. No disrespect was meant."

They moved past Steadfast, almost shoving him aside, clearly not afraid of the uniform or helmet. These two were professionals alright, thought Steadfast, professional hoodlums.

"Pretty," said Lynch, looking at Abrasia as he would a mule to be bought.

"If you say so," said Schism. He addressed Steadfast: "We have a carriage waiting outside."

"There was one thing that I meant to ask," said Steadfast. "How does Wheldrake expect to hide the fact that my lady's body has disappeared. He said that you had it in hand."

"Indeed we do. Lynch, kindly transfer our lady to the carriage and bring in the other package."

Studying his nails and humming, Schism let his grunting partner do the heavy lifting. Abrasia's hand swung, her feet dangled limp as the ogre in a crumpled hat carried her away. Steadfast felt his heart lurch as if it were attached by string to Abrasia's ankle; yanked out, and dragged into the alleyway behind her, never to be seen again. He rubbed at his chest as if to ease the sensation.

Lynch returned with a sack, heavily stained and stinking of rot. Steadfast pressed a glove to his nose.

As the sack was opened, Steadfast turned away.

Sounds of rummaging and movement.

As morbid curiosity made Steadfast return, Lynch was replacing the lid of the coffin.

"See? All taken care of," said Schism, dusting his hands as if he had done the work.

"What if someone opens the coffin?" asked

Steadfast.

"Don't let them."

Schism and Lynch left Steadfast alone with the coffin.

He prayed. He prayed to whatever God was on duty.

He prayed hard and long.

25

How to extract Loosestrife from the lab had been Wheldrake's greatest problem. He'd planned to conjure an invitation for the Professor, maybe invite him to the Academe on behalf of the scholars. He'd accept the invitation, there was no doubt about that; Loosestrife never passed up an opportunity to patronise other scientists. He would arrive and, due to their justified fear for the old reaper, they wouldn't question his arrival. And he'd never acknowledge why he was there in case they thought he was easily summoned. It was a good plan.

But when Wheldrake returned from his final errand, exhausted by two nights of feverish planning and secret work, Loosestrife had already gone. There was only a note left on one of the benches:

I am out. I will return in no longer than two days.

The fates had twice blessed Wheldrake's venture. He had no idea where Loosestrife would go for that long. He had no family, having been spawned from some cesspit as far as Wheldrake knew. Certainly no friends.

It would be sinister, no doubt, and Wheldrake would pay for it later. But for now he thanked his luck, the Gods and Fate.

Now there was only the waiting.

Wheldrake sat in the laboratory's green gloom, his body thrumming like a plucked cello. He paced, a screwdriver twirling in his fingers for the minor distraction it gave. Finally he went through to the anteroom.

Twice he answered the door, imagining the bell's jingle, and returned to his seat.

Another hour.

The bell came again. This time in reality. He stiffened.

Schism stood in the alley with his grin; a friendly invitation to doom. As Wheldrake answered, Schism motioned to his partner. Lynch leapt down from a carriage at the end of the alley. Propped on the seat was a beautiful corpse. Wheldrake swallowed the heart out of this throat.

Lynch grumbled as he dragged Abrasia's body from the carriage.

Wheldrake clenched his tiny teeth.

The Brawn of the unlawful partnership held the girl over his shoulder; a monster carrying a captured damsel.

Wheldrake passed a large bag to the silent Schism; it was twice the size it should have been.

"Most generous," said Schism. "Are you sure that there's no other function you want us to perform for the sum?"

Wheldrake nodded, knowing that the wily crook was onto him.

"Silence," he said.

"That won't be a problem."

Schism motioned to Lynch who passed the girl's body over. He cracked his spine backward with pleasure and a groan once she was in Wheldrake's arms, who held her without flinching at the weight.

Lynch mumbled something.

"Good evening, gentlemen," said Wheldrake.

"Good evening, Professor," said Schism, doffing his cap as the door closed.

Wheldrake ignored the comment and, to release the tension, he ran. His coat tails flapped as he whisked down the corridor and out into the lab, Abrasia's head nestled to his shoulder. When he lowered her to the bench it was with all the care he could muster, feeling that he didn't have enough hands to support every part of her limp torso that he should.

The dank green light and eerie shapes surrounding her made Abrasia seem celestial by comparison; a cherub with harsh features. Wheldrake wanted to remove her from this place more than ever. He grasped two chains that hung out of the darkness and heaved.

The Womb rose.

Guiding the contraption through the air, swinging on the chains with cautious haste, he lowered it beside Abrasia with a clang.

The girl didn't flinch. Wheldrake froze.

This was the point when he had to be sure. He hadn't told Steadfast the final stage of his plan for fear that the Captain wouldn't understand, but this was the most safety that Wheldrake could give the heiress.

He stepped back, paused, and then lifted her.

There was no rise and fall of her chest against him. For a moment, Wheldrake faltered. He pressed his fingers to her throat. Nothing, of course.

Stood in the dark of the laboratory, Wheldrake shook himself.

"If you carry on like this, you'll never finish," he said to the darkness.

He'd never been under so much pressure that he couldn't stand it. But there was something about this, something that resonated on a higher frequency of importance. If he were a religious man, he might have thought it divine.

The Womb's lid slotted into place and handles twisted with a *clunk*.

He screwed the Elixir's sloshing canisters into the base of The Womb and watched through the small window as the girl began to float, and then was submerged in the liquid. There was no struggling this time; no pleading like there had been with Albert Snitch.

Wheldrake folded against The Womb for a moment, feeling the cool metal on his face.

Grasping the chains once more, he leapt up onto The Womb like an acrobat. He stood wide legged and, bracing himself for movement, yanked hard. The Womb and Wheldrake rose into space. Crossing the room together, weaving between the other mechanical blasphemies in the semi-dark, they came to rest against the laboratory's wall. Wheldrake leapt down without making a sound on the hollow flooring. In what seemed like an instant, the chains swung free and Wheldrake had The Womb on the brink of the disposal chute.

He didn't pause to think.

With a final heave, The Womb drifted downward until the shadows swallowed it whole and then was lost.

It was done. If Abrasia was to be truly safe from discovery, the impossible maze of sewers below the city would be the place to hide her.

The chute's lid squeaked closed.

Wheldrake's breath escaped in a shudder. He slid down the wall, eyes closed, and let himself dwindle into the darkness.

Darrant stood on the pipe's brink and looked out. Exiting half way up the Greaveburn Wall, the pipe sprayed water into thin air above the eastern swamp. Enormous vines made a complex scaffolding up to the pipe, wrapping their tendrils around the outlet. There had been rain the night before, rendering the sprawling woods below a lush green. A fresh wind surprised Darrant with its scent. Even from this vantage, he couldn't see anything he thought might be Vale. He ducked back into the pipe, feeling light headed from the clean air.

"It's a long way down," he said.

"*cfgh* There are other ways, but I thought you'd like *cfgh* to see it first," said Joseph.

"I can't see anything. Just trees and more trees."

Joseph stepped to the edge and extended a finger.

"Where the *cfgh* hill rises, there's a break in the trees. Not there. Further north. There'll be a lake. It's not easy to find."

"I'll find it," said Darrant but with the same determination that had failed him when searching for the Broken Folk in his previous life.

"You're smiling *cfgh*."

Darrant reached back for a cloth package tied with twine. Placing it at the small of his back, he wrapped the twine like a belt so that his arms would be free. Steadfast's sword was wrapped in rags and already strapped across his back.

"I was thinking about pride."

"And that makes you smile? I'll never understand you, Riccall."

"Thank the Gods for that," he said. He took Joseph's hand and shook it. "I better get started if I'm to make the most of the light. Take care of everyone while I'm gone."

"I only brought you here to give you directions, Riccall. You can't possibly-" Joseph cut himself short. Darrant was testing the nearest vine with his foot and smiling as well as his face would allow.

Darrant turned to his friend and flexed his fingerless hand.

"I think it's ready for the challenge." He looked over

the edge. "I suppose it won't take long to find out if I'm right."

"You're insane," said Joseph, holding his head as if the very thought of climbing down gave him a migraine.

"Not yet," said Darrant. "But I'm getting there."

He swung himself out onto the vines, and out of Greaveburn.

26

Corwater rounded the corner of Gracen Street, where the theatre district began with smaller, independent houses. Between the hand-painted signs of those cheaper theatres, acres of bleak wall were covered in layer upon layer of mouldering posters; a visual history of Greaveburn's performing arts in paper and paste. It was easy to imagine that there was no wall underneath at all and that the whole area was made of the same ancient papier-mâché as a stage landscape. Outside some of the theatres the ropes had been removed, but cordon bollards still marked where people usually queued. But not tonight.

Today, Greaveburn was insufferable; devoid of even a sprinkle of life. The few people Corwater did see were mute and low-faced. Stood by a pile of newspapers almost his own height, a boy brandished a copy to passers-by. The cover image was a single portrait. A dead girl rendered in sepia. Such a shame, but inevitable, it seemed. Corwater tried not to think about it much but everywhere he looked, all enjoyment had been sucked out of his city by the last Glenhaven's untimely death. Here in the theatre district, there was always music, any time of the day. But not today. The taverns were still open, of course, but all the noise and sweat was gone. And by stage doors, actors pale with greasepaint smoked their cigarettes in silence.

After the smaller houses came the Primas Theatre with its bowed facade. Corwater passed the glass-shielded posters at street level, each one struck through with a single word. Cancelled. He huffed, and flicked the glass. Of course, it *was* a tragedy, but why ruin everyone else's day? He moved on, hunting the streets for something, anything to amuse him. Since his altercation with Grinda Choler, he'd stayed out of the way and that meant attending Lady Abrasia's funeral was out of the question. If only because he couldn't bear the snide look the old crow would be wearing.

Beckoning to a cab, he stepped back from the curb to avoid the splash of mud on his shoes.

"Destination, Lordship?" asked the well-wrapped driver from his perch behind the horses.

"Wherever the wind takes you, my man. Let your horses lead."

The driver nodded. Corwater flicked open the carriage's latch with his cane before climbing in. The inside still smelled heavily of the previous occupant; sweat musk and cheap perfume, a man and his nightly entertainment. Corwater sniffed it out of his nose. Sliding a hand into his pocket, he took out the bill he'd found tucked into his letterbox that morning. He twitched aside the carriage's curtain and leaned so he could see by the light. A small sheet, hastily prepared with ink that ran and spellings that changed every time he read it. Still, the message seemed heartfelt. He read the leaflet again; more a letter of threat to those in power. It hadn't taken long for rumours to spread that the Cholers' had employed foul-play to cause Abrasia's death, and now someone was wishing justice on the Archduke. The leaflet swore vengeance, promised hell, and said it would come from a thousand directions at once. Corwater doubted the last part. Peasants were so quick to shout and late to stand. Organisation was what they fundamentally lacked. No doubt nothing would come of it. He folded the leaflet back into his pocket and stabbed the ceiling with his cane. A slot opened in the wall above his head with the driver's face behind it.

"Lordship?"

"Take me to the Temple, I feel like going shopping."

The journey passed with a gentle rocking that lulled Corwater almost into a light doze. It was such a shame he never got the chance to meet the girl, Abrasia. He'd always admired her from a distance; the last thing to stand against Grinda Choler's plans for ruling Greaveburn when Legat eventually died. A beautiful little thorn in the old dog's paw. In his half sleep, Corwater chuckled.

The carriage leaned into an upward slope as it began to climb Temple Hill toward the ancient building which was now a shopping arcade. Corwater peered out of the window at the rich houses without really seeing them. From beyond the carriage's wall, the driver gave a sharp curse. The horses whinnied, and Corwater's head slammed the wall as the carriage slid to a halt. The slot above his head slid open.

"Sorry, Sir. Had to make a quick stop. There's some disturbance in the road ahead. Best to stay inside. I think."

Patting down his hair, Corwater swung open the door and stepped onto the cobbles. Other carriages and solo riders were drawing to a halt around him, pale faces peering out but none daring to emerge fully. Stomping hooves and startled nickering filled the street as horses were spooked by the commotion up ahead. The driver had been right. Corwater moved toward it, not entirely sure what he was seeing. There were people, maybe hundreds, clustered in the road; a mass of brown and grey with dirty faces. He couldn't make out their shouts but it was a rhythmic, pulsing chant. Some held up boards scrawled with paint, others held crumpled papers high like weapons.

A mob. A protest in the streets of the inner city. The upper class were being forced from their carriages and onto the pavements by small groups of angry individuals. Corwater took the initiative to move before they reached him. Around him, the upper classes whimpered and clutched at each other. A woman passed him, a maid judging by her dirty pinafore. Thrusting a leaflet into his hand, she moved along like a worker bee pollinating with propaganda. The paper was similar to the one he already had. There were more angry words in this version, and red ink had been bought for the cause. The shouting grew to an almighty volume, drawing his eye upward.

Behind Lieutenant Cawber, the City Guard were arriving.

Elbowing top hats and bonnets aside, Corwater moved up onto a house's steps for a better view. The Guard had truncheons drawn and were trying to hem the mob, but it was a pulsing, living thing now and every peasant had become part of the larger organism. A shattering scream rattled nearby windows. Corwater snapped his head around just in time to see the first missile thrown. The bottle whipped over the guards' heads, brown glass refracting the sunlight in a murky glow. And as its shards exploded across the cobbles, all hell broke loose.

Corwater bit on his glove to stop from giggling. It seemed he was wrong. Greaveburn was about to become more interesting than he'd ever hoped.

Part II

27

Stars wheeled before Cluracan's squint as if trying to avoid his gaze. With fingers like gnarled tree roots he adjusted the focus. A complex scattering of stars formed before his age-whitened eye.

He watched for a while, gently scanning this way and that, and finally settled on a constellation he'd been admiring for some months. Never before had he seen so much activity in the stars; so much that they swung and bobbed like baubles. There was a convergence in those glimmering shards; something he'd failed to foresee despite his constant skyward attention.

A sharp intake of breath.

Cluracan shot back from the telescope.

Fumbling at his charts, knocking some to the floor in the process, he found what he was looking for. It had been near the bottom of the pile, as he'd expected. It was nearly two years since it had been drawn. Back when Cluracan had his last visitor. Back before Abrasia was lost. He held the chart so close to his face that a smudge of charcoal stained his bulbous beak of a nose.

Rusty squeaks of a mouse choir issued from the

ceiling and walls as the telescope swung around on its rail.

Cluracan looked through the viewing eyelet. Looked again. Checked the chart.

He sat back as far as the curved lump of his spine would allow.

"Oh dear."

Fibrous tendrils hung like candelabra, obscuring the view of anything more than a few feet ahead. A figure picked its way through the foliage, twisting its course to follow the sound of running water nearby. Its robe was a swathe of tattered cloth, disguising the figure's true shape with untidy humps and frays.

A smell had begun to attack him as he followed the river's course; the putrid breath of a carrion beast. From beneath the ragged cowl a deep, shivering inhalation. It was the smell of home.

Coming to a halt, the figure swayed backward, extended something three fingers shy of a hand. Greaveburn's wall extended so high that only clouds could pass over. Vines adhered to the enormous stones like veins beneath sickened skin. The man once known as Darrant traced the faint edges of masonry with a trembling palm.

Following the wall, he tracked the sound of gurgling. Water burbled out of a broken pipe wide enough to take a chariot down its centre. Despite the growing stench, he didn't hesitate, but ducked inside. Disappearing from the swamp's writhing world of green and half-light, Riccall returned to the cloying gloom of Greaveburn's sewers.

28

Sunlight bled through the heavy oak blinds, filling Lord Happenstance's library with murky light. Happenstance himself stood so ram-rod straight that he leant slightly backward, his fists resting at the small of his back. Facing the blinds, he was lit in stripes from head to foot. He looked out at the lice-filled mattress that was Greaveburn through glazed eyes.

Corwater reclined in a deep armchair, enjoying the feel of the soft leather. A silver tipped cane rolled between his delicate fingers. The rebellious Choler felt no remorse for fraternising with Lord Happenstance despite the Lord's Glenhaven allegiances. After all, there was no Glenhaven left to align himself to and hadn't been for a long time. Since Abrasia died, Happenstance was a nonentity in the fragile equilibrium of Greaveburn society; a neutral.

"Staring at it won't make it any better," Corwater said.

The elder gentleman made a slight sound. An acknowledgement, or the clearing of a throat. It was so slight that Corwater might have imagined it.

"I said…"

"I often think that nothing will make it better," came Happenstance's sullen break to a three hour silence. "It would be far better that this place sink back into the swamp."

"Happenstance, you're such a wet lettuce and an almost insufferable bore at times."

Lord Happenstance finally turned to regard Corwater. The youth was certainly striking, almost feline, having little of his family's over-shared blood. And he used the most entertaining slang Happenstance had ever heard.

"Maybe I am," said Happenstance. The smile, nothing more than another wrinkle on his face. "At least I see the problem as it is rather than hiding from it."

"My dear Lord, I hope you're not insinuating that I hide from anything. I am what I am and those who disapprove are welcome to a piece of my tongue."

"And a finely sharpened one it is too."

Corwater gave a mock wave of gratitude. Happenstance took a final, longing look at his city, and turned away.

29

Riccall emerged from the alleyway and tore a leaflet from the rotting notice board. There were no Wanted posters here, only images of the people already captured and their supposed crimes.

"How long?" he asked.

"Almost *cfgh* six months," said the little man by his side.

"Bastards."

Joseph remained silent but *cfgh*ed agreement.

"Are they ours?" asked Riccall.

"Some are, most *cfgh* aren't. The riots went on for almost a year-"

"And the riots started after-" he pressed a hand to his forehead "-just after she died. I always knew what the Archduke intended but never really thought he'd dare. Damn him and that horde of his."

Darrant screwed the poster tight in his good hand. He felt like tearing at it with his teeth, savaging it and not stopping until the Citadel lay burning at his feet. He'd left to buy time, settle his mind. When he returned, Abrasia would be grown, ready for her coronation, and he'd be there to make sure it happened.

Tears rolled down his face from his good eye. The scarred side had long since been incapable.

Joseph looked up and down the street, over his shoulder. They were too close to the Shackles' edge here. He patted Riccall on the shoulder. Joseph had no idea that his friend would be so upset by the deaths.

"There's nothing *cfgh* we could do. Not even you. The riots *cfgh* broke when the Inspectors starting arresting people. That *cfgh* kind of news gets around. The arrests still carry on, even now *cfgh*."

Darrant choked back his tears, but his voice came thick when he spoke again.

"Fear works, Joseph. Everyone's scared of something. These Inspectors have made sure it's them. But who are they? And how have they managed to overtake the Guard?"

"The Archduke," said Joseph.

"Legat Choler is a paranoid coward. A string-puller. The most he ever did was write a letter. But these Inspectors; torturers in uniform, they're something else. Some*one* else. Someone who wants the peasants washed away, even if they use rivers of blood to do it. To think, I almost didn't come back," said Riccall. With a weak smile he turned to his friend and laid a hand on his shoulder. "Of course, I would have come to visit you."

"Oh, yes, I'm sure you would."

"You didn't '*cfgh*' " said Riccall.

"The sarcasm scared it away."

They dissolved into the Shackles' brown backdrop. Winding through a lattice of cramped alleyways, sometimes squeezing sideways between hovels, they rounded a shack's dishevelled mass and found the sewer cover.

"The Inspectors are paying people with food to *cfgh* tattle on their neighbours. No one can resist," said Joseph. His voice began to echo as they descended.

"The trade *cfgh* routes in and out of the Shackles have been *cfgh* closed too long. Any food that was stored is gone. They're *cfgh*-oping that everyone will turn *cfgh* on us when it gets too much."

"It isn't about us anymore. It's about Greaveburn. Everyone has the same stake in the city's future, whether Broken or not. The Shackles is the first place to realise it because you helped them see. Others will follow in time. Choler is pushing too hard for them not to," said Riccall.

He hopped the last few feet where the moss-slick ladder fell short, his boots splashing in sewage.

"That doesn't help us now," reasoned Joseph. "We're starving."

"There's plenty of food," said Riccall. "We just have to be prepared to take it. Not to worry, Joseph, I'm back now. Get everyone together. Things are going to change around here."

YOU are the Broken Ones

It appeared overnight, all across Greaveburn. Corwater saw it daubed in greasy paint across the theatre district's poster wall. Steadfast found it scratched into the guard house's door frame. Cluracan looked down from his tower and twisted his head to read the uneven script daubed on the road outside the palace.

And in the Shackles, another message. Two words in red paint as if etched in blood.

Rise Up.

30

Steadfast sat at his desk, fingers knotted into his hair.

Reports from last year's riots towered over him in paper pillars to rival the Citadel. There had to be something to help him find Riccall, somewhere in all that paper. Riccall remained an enigma. There were no roots, no family, no friends to interrogate. He simply didn't exist, for all of Steadfast's trying. Some said he lived beneath the city with the outcasts, or he was a carpenter from the Artisan's Quarter, huddled beneath the Greaveburn Belfry. Neither had brought any viable leads. Riccall was clever. There was nothing Steadfast hated more than a clever villain. At least brutal, greedy and bitter men made mistakes. Riccall's activities had begun with small assaults on guard houses, defacement and suchlike, but soon the guard were stretched too thin to cope. Rumour had it that some of the Broken Folk had crept back into the city.

The situation was intolerable for Archduke Choler, and more importantly for his sister. The Archduke's mind had soured. The death of Lady Abrasia and simultaneous disappearance of Professor Loosestrife turned inquisitive eyes toward the Archduke. Pressure was rising. For a man whose idea of coping with confrontation was to buy a bigger wardrobe to hide in, things looked bad. The Archduke's only saviour was Grinda.

Archduke Legat Choler had been crowned monarch a week after Abrasia's death, retaining the title of Archduke out of false respect for his 'ill-fated' adversaries. The coronation was a sordid affair in his private quarters, kept secret for the most part. A priest was brought in, literally on his death bed, by two assistants, a stretcher laid on the floor, and the ceremony performed by proxy. His understudy was a twitchy young man, and he had reason; Grinda Choler and her vulturous daughters were in attendance. The Archduke huddled in his chair like a startled raccoon, Grinda standing sentinel at his side, her claw almost pinning him to the seat. The whining sisters bickered and hissed like sausages. Before returning to his duties, Steadfast had called a medic for the old priest, who had died noisily toward the middle of the ceremony.

Steadfast slid another sheet of paper from the pile of reports in front of him and began to sign without reading. The new recruit's training regimes had to be confirmed before Barghest could get them underway. This was the first step to fighting back against Riccall's rebels. New recruits. Boys. And Steadfast had the job of handing them their badges; the Hangman's handshake.

Shoving the reports aside, Steadfast grabbed for his helmet.

It was a long walk to the edge of the Shackles. He passed through the inner city's boundary on his way. The south gate had once been an arch of such size that four carriages could have passed through abreast with two further balanced on their roofs. Its catastrophic collapse at the end of the last century had been caused by a descendant of the original architect trying to prove exactly how sturdy it was. Where they had landed, enormous pieces of frieze-decorated rock still lay. The Lord's body was supposedly still beneath one of them. History had forgotten which.

Between the ancient stones hung heavy canopies of deepest blue, grey and khaki mingled into a patchwork ceiling. A complex cloud of aromas swirled in invisible eddies beneath. Bundles of garlic hung from stall posts; chives, coriander and thyme were snipped straight from the plant; turmeric and chilli were bartered over enthusiastically according to their rarity. The Greaveburn Pound switched hands faster than a glance could measure.

The spice market was one of Greaveburn's busiest commercial areas. When the diet of a city was so reliant on cabbages and potatoes grown on the western plains, it was no wonder the populace craved anything that would add taste. Of all the things that can be said of Greaveburners (despite their seemingly reckless disregard for one another's wellbeing and predisposition to nefarious activity) they were experts in the delicate manipulation of spice and herb.

Steadfast shouldered through the market's throng, feeling the weight of people's hatred as surely as he felt their physical presence. Heavy gazes lingered too long; children were hushed as they tried to repeat something their father had said; the crowd didn't part for him as quickly as it should.

He understood.

The blue of his uniform wasn't his skin, underneath he was as pink as the rest of them. Beneath his helmet was the worried brain of a Greaveburner.

The peasants had forced the Guard out of the Shackles in one short month. Ambushes in the cramped streets and dead ends were impossible to counter. The Broken Folk were on the roofs, in the sewers; they seemed to be coming from the damn walls. Steadfast was responsible for every failed attempt the Guard made to reclaim it. That was why he'd stopped trying. It was safer to remove his men completely than watch them be massacred.

Brand Street had become the border between Greaveburn and the Shackles, and then a stage. The play was called Intimidation.

Steadfast shaded his eyes from the sun, and heaved a sigh.

Their chains creaking like whale song, cages filled with tattered human remains swung from gibbets all along Brand Street, their rotting inhabitants held captive between heaven and earth for eternity. An example had been made, a statement of Choler solidarity.

A maelstrom of feather, claw and beak raged above Steadfast's head. The ravens had come from all over the city, hungry for free meat. Even now, with no captures for over a week, they hovered, visible from all over Greaveburn as a permanent blemish on the sky. Steadfast stared upward, losing himself in their swirling masses for a moment.

He thanked the Gods that he had nothing to do with this atrocity. A new kind of policeman was responsible. Cawber had been promoted and given the title of Chief Inspector. His Inspectors were a law unto themselves. They had their own offices, their own cells; they had cellars and dark places, and spies. They employed men with surgeon's skill and a devil's morals. But of the rebels captured, their success rate was exemplary. Not a single person they arrested had been found innocent.

The caged dead of Brand Street were all that was left of the Inspectors' victims.

Steadfast moved on, trying not to skid in the raven droppings that scarred the cobbles of Brand Street. Today, he had to be elsewhere, and he was grateful for it.

31

Sergeant Barghest stood to attention outside the Archduke's office; the pouch of his gut and tilt of his helmet making him a slovenly statue.

This part of his job was purely decorative. The Archduke never left his quarters anymore, the office being used more often by his sister, Grinda. Barghest didn't think about it much. The job was nice and easy. Sliding his way toward retirement, his thoughts mostly surrounded the six foot square patch that he called a garden and when the next cigarette was coming. He made it his business to never hear anything that happened inside the office, despite the fact that the door was quite thin and his hearing exceptional. Just then, he wasn't hearing the bickering of the Grinda Choler and her daughters.

"Will you two shut up!" bellowed Grinda.

The girls, so engrossed in their quarrel, didn't hear her until she stood right behind them. Her ever-cold talons gripped their bare shoulders until they yelped like pups.

"I said, silence," she hissed.

Whimpering, the girls lowered their voices.

"What bothers you so, Mummy?" asked Frina, the elder sister, when she dared.

"This Wheldrake character." Grinda once more set about her papers.

"What of him?"

"He was Loosestrife's apprentice."

"He looks funny," offered Ayles.

"*You* look funny," mumbled Frina.

"Mummy, she said I look funny-"

Recognising the rise of another argument, Grinda spoke on reflex. "Shut up, both of you." After a sigh, she continued: "I wonder if he's trustworthy."

"Was Professor Loosestrife trustworthy?" asked Frina.

"No. But I could always trust him to be untrustworthy when I needed him to be. Wheldrake on the other hand is far too trustworthy to be trusted."

Watching her sister's brow furrow, Frina saw another opportunity.

"Do try to keep up Ayles. I know it's difficult."

"I'm sure I don't know what you mean."

"That's my point, you never do."

"Mummy, she said I don't unde-"

"SHUT UP BOTH OF YOU."

Outside the door, Barghest heard nothing at all, and flinched.

"Mummy? You said that when Uncle Legat got too poorly to rule, that I could take over. You said it was in the bloodline. I want to be Queen!" said Ayles. At the age of twenty two, Ayles hadn't been courted once. It wasn't for the sake of her looks. For a Choler, she wasn't too dastardly looking. Her tiny little nose with its upturned tip made her look as if she were constantly testing the air, but that could be overlooked. She just had enough whine in her voice to run her own vineyard.

"I changed my mind," said Grinda.

"It's because you're an imbecile," Frina said to her

sister. She tugged at her shawl in the long mirror so that it slipped slightly, exposing just a little too much of her bosom; better that a man's eye be drawn downward and away from her face.

"If I rule, that would leave you free to go and ... kiss all those boys you like so much."

Frina's eyes grew slim and her mouth stern. She whispered: "Why, you little brat."

"Shut up, both of you," a tired edge had risen in Grinda's voice. "And, Frina? Remind me to speak to you later."

Ayle's meat-red tongue darted out from between her lips.

32

"No, Riccall. No."

Lattices of green light swam over every surface; faces became masks of obscene movement. If they remained still, no-one would be able to tell the Broken Folk from the jumble that filled their makeshift home.

Mrs Foible continued:

"You can *not* take us to war over food, Riccall." She leaned in close to him, so that the others couldn't hear.

"You're right, wars are fought for *much* better reasons." He rubbed the scarred side of his face. It still itched, even now.

"Don't test your wit on me, boy-" said Mrs Foible. Birgit approached, cutting her short.

The young woman placed a brown mug beside Mrs Foible so that it could cool. To Riccall she handed an earthenware bowl without scowl or squint. Birgit's hatred for him had lost its keen edge, it seemed, but the blade was still strong. When he thanked her she nodded civilly. Retreating across the swaying platform, Birgit took her seat beside Narelle. Riccall watched as she teased hair back over her scarred face before settling in to soothe the child to sleep. As Narelle nuzzled into her lap, Birgit went to turn down the light. Her hand faltered short of the lamp's flame, and she withdrew. Joseph reached across from his seat, turning the lamp down to a glimmer without a word.

Riccall came back to the conversation smiling, but aware that he'd missed a part of Mrs Foible's speech.

"-a smattering of mutants and cripples, not an army."

"I know that. But we're starving. Not just the Broken Ones, but the rest of the Shackles, too." He blew into his tea, taking in a scent that reminded him of tilled earth.

She lifted his chin so that he was forced to meet her silver gaze.

"You're using our plight to exact your revenge, Riccall. Are you willing to sacrifice us all for your own sake? Or are you truly trying to help in the only way you know how?"

Riccall met her eyes, but only briefly before returning to his tea.

"As I thought," she said. "I can't stop you, nor can I stop anyone from following you. But know that I'll forever hold you responsible for what you're about to do."

33

Wheldrake stepped out onto Ginnal Avenue, peeling a damp cobweb from his sleeve. He looked both ways, checking that no one had seen him. It was harder to sneak around now so many people knew his face.

Since Loosestrife's 'disappearance', Wheldrake had tried to adapt The Womb's design to cure The Ague. He soon realised that resources for the elixir were too scarce, and the process too slow. By the time anyone was cured, ten others would be infected. Over months of careful testing, he'd linked The Ague to a single source. Three wells, all inter-connected, that fed water to most of the lower areas of Greaveburn. Unable to climb the great wall, the swamp had dug its roots underneath until most of Eastern Greaveburn now sprouted vines through the cobbles. The same tendrils infiltrated the network of tunnels that connected those three wells and all manner of creatures and moulds came with it.

The solution had been so simple in design but long in construction.

Where the river Greave encircled the northern edge

of the city before leaking into the swamp at the east, pipes had been laid to redirect the water. They ran down most major streets, lined with hand pumps like brass spines. They weren't pretty, and hadn't cured The Ague completely (only complete eradication of the vines would see to that), but the numbers of the sick and dying had slowed to a trickle. And with every life saved, Wheldrake felt a sin washed away.

Grinda Choler, of course, had claimed the triumph in the name of her brother.

Wheldrake turned sharply, leaving the avenue.

Across a small square, Steadfast waited beneath the cloister.

"I'd point out that you're late, but I'd be stating the obvious and it'd make no difference," said Steadfast.

Wheldrake regarded the Captain, head cocked to one side and a wry smile on his lips. Steadfast crossed his arms to hide the hairs that stood to attention.

"If you want the best of company, it's worth waiting for," said Wheldrake.

They stood together in silence, looking up and regarding Greaveburn Belfry, reduced to pastel colours by the haze of distance.

"How could we build something so magnificent and end up where we are?" asked Steadfast.

"There's a certain element of necessity involved, I think," said Wheldrake. He scratched behind his ear, tipping his head to the side, and studied the evidence in his fingernails. "'We' built such catastrophes of architecture to prove that we could. But once the point is proven, why continue?"

"But the Belfry is a thousand years old-"

"Older," added Wheldrake.

"-so why haven't we tried something even more impressive?"

"Lack of imagination? Inferiority complex? Preoccupied with holding our fellow humans beneath a yolk of tyrannical oppression?" suggested Wheldrake with a tiny-toothed smile.

"Something like that," said Steadfast, purposefully not looking at his companion's grin.

They were no longer alone.

Steadfast and Wheldrake sank back into the shadow of the cloister.

Entering the square was an old woman towing a cart behind her. The vehicle waddled like a pregnant clown, constantly in jeopardy of shedding its load. Rolls of material were piled high, and more still were across the old woman's back. A small child rode in a sling around her chest.

Shrill battle cries and wails of pretend war echoed back and forth across the square. Five dirt-encrusted children appeared in the old woman's wake. Each carried some kind of baton; a broken branch, a broom handle or a strip of mouldered wood. As Steadfast and Wheldrake watched, the children caught up with the cart and began beating it, advancing and falling back, ducking beneath imaginary talons or yelping at the scorch of fiery breath. The cart took a beating but the old woman ignored her ware's assailants until one of the rolls was knocked loose. The crone hobbled about like a crippled seal. She hissed through naked gums.

The children froze, petrified.

"Get away you urchins!" she screeched. "Away with you and leave me be."

The children drew back, chastised, except one who presented a vertical index finger to the crone before running away.

"*BASTARDS!*" yelled the old crone, drawing out her vowels with venom.

Bending further forward, she placed the baby on the moss-coated cobbles. Cooing and muttering assurances, she repacked her cart in the same haphazard fashion as before. Soon she was back on her way with the baby swinging beneath her sagging breast.

"What was it this time?" Wheldrake asked when Steadfast didn't take up the conversation.

"This time I'm him and he's me. He speaks to me, words that I don't understand or can't hear, and then he skewers me. I fall into the sewer opening and I feel hands grabbing at me in the dark. Then I wake up. For a moment after I wake up, I can still feel the blade. Just for a moment."

"Do you really need me to explain?" asked Wheldrake.

"No. Of course not."

"It's simple guilt, Captain. It will lessen and pass in time," said Wheldrake. He raised his hand to place it on the Captain's shoulder, and thought better of it.

"It's been so long already, and I only get worse." Steadfast removed his helmet and smoothed his hair.

"If it's forgiveness you want, go to the Cathedral and pray to the Gods. But I assure you, they won't answer. They never do. You've performed your act of contrition. A life saved for a life destroyed. Surely that should be enough."

"You'd think so, wouldn't you?" said Steadfast.

The laboratory was only partially lit. Wheldrake found the lack of light helped him to think, like closing the eyes improves hearing or sense of smell.

He found his way through the darkness by intuition, listening to the *plink* of his tread on steel. He hadn't removed any of his predecessor's contraptions from the room. He was bent on turning even the smallest component to his advantage. The more of Loosestrife's creations he could cannibalise, the more of the Professor's evil would be undone.

With a cure for The Ague underway, he'd turned his mind to bringing the power of the eels, which Loosestrife had guarded so selfishly, to the streets above.

Finding his seat by the workstation, Wheldrake

closed his eyes.

There would need to be a station built. Somewhere central that housed the eels, and even bred-

"Always thinking and never doing."

The voice was cracked like plaster, damp.

"Be quiet Professor," said Wheldrake. "I'm not in the mood."

"Oh, I apologise for breaking your concentration. I know how difficult it is for you to string coherent thought together."

"Just be quiet."

There was silence, a moment or two that seemed longer in the dark.

"I am hungry," said the Professor.

Wheldrake stood with a sigh.

A whisper of hinges, a thud, scraping.

Lights flickered, giving off a thick click with each flash, and lit.

Carrying a plate across the lab, Wheldrake reached inside the shadowed alcove.

Zzzzzub zzzub zubzub. The overhead light came on.

Legs tucked clumsily under him, Professor Loosestrife sat on the floor of the alcove. One arm stretched upward and wrenched uncomfortably around; thick iron bars pierced his artificial forearm and locked into the stone of the alcove's wall at top and bottom.

If he wanted to, Loosestrife had the ability to release himself. All he had to do was remove the arm and slide free. But Wheldrake was confident that his ego wouldn't let him even contemplate it.

Wheldrake placed the plate of miscellaneous food on the ground and slid it over with his foot.

Loosestrife screwed up his haggard face. His hair was wild at one side where he rested it to sleep; dirt clogged his wrinkles, deepening them. His tiny red eyes had lost nothing of their intensity but had gained heavy baggage.

"Hardly hygienic," he muttered, but began to delve into the pile of food with his free hand. He shifted things aside, nibbling on a morsel only to trade it for another.

"Satisfied?" asked Wheldrake.

"You know what would satisfy me," he said. Raising a scrap of meat to his lips, he glared at Wheldrake from beneath thundercloud brows. The meat tore between Loosestrife's teeth, a droplet of juice ran down his lip.

Wheldrake didn't answer. The glare made him nauseous.

"How long do you intend to hold me here?" continued the Professor conversationally. "Can you not gather the spine to kill me? Or does it please you to see a man tortured?"

Turning to leave, Wheldrake said: "Eat your dinner."

Loosestrife slid the plate away.

A cloying sweet scent; a sharp taste of ether in his throat; the burning in his twisted shoulder bringing him to full, horrifying consciousness. Loosestrife remembered the moment he woke in captivity so vividly that his head swam as it had then.

His stomach was a dried walnut. It grumbled to him.

He could smell himself. The musk of old sweat and reek of his own waste sank into his clothing, skin and bone. If there was ever a release, he'd never feel clean again. His nose would remember, of that he was certain.

Immersing himself in the laboratory's dark, Loosestrife let it hide his shame. He winced, bringing himself to his knees in preparation for working on the bars. At first he'd torn at them like a captured animal, yelling outrage and fear, but that served only to wrench his shoulder further; his rage lost in the darkness. After the red curtain of panic lifted, Loosestrife's clockwork mind had asserted itself. Now he pried at the bars with slow deliberation, twisting this way and that, trying to work them free. In moments of desperate hallucination he'd felt them twist, or bend, or lift, only to realise it was a slip of his hand on the metal.

He regarded the oozing abrasions on his palm, flexed its worn flesh. The heat of friction had begun to sear his battered nerves but still he continued to twist and rattle the bar.

At first he dismissed it as an illusion of useless hope, until it happened again. Wiping fresh blood on his soiled and thinning trousers, Loosestrife winced at the sensation of glass in his palm. Still, he reached out once more to test his brain's deception.

Beneath the grip of his tacky palm, so slight as to be unrecognisable to anyone but himself, the bar shifted in its socket.

34

Dense nebulas of steam rolled against the low ceiling. Exposed timbers were vaguely recognisable through the swirling fog; the shadows of sharks above a trapped diver. Girls in cloth caps bustled through the kitchen's aisles with mops and cloths. Pots boiled and bubbled with nothing but water inside, their lids adding a low rattle to the backdrop of sound. It was a long while since it had been necessary to cook anything in the palace kitchens, but Mama Carnale liked to maintain a working environment.

She stood at a long table, sloshing thick soup into three bowls.

"Are we going to be sacked?" asked the youngest of the group, a boy of no more than twelve.

"To be honest, son, I don't think they care enough to sack us," said his father.

The third man slumbered, his thin whiskers resting on his chest, and grumbled in his sleep.

"Three generations of tasters with nothing to taste," the father continued. "What have we come to?"

"Not to worry Jared, not to worry," said Mrs

Carnale, handing him a bowl of soup. "I'm sure it won't last forever."

Jared shook his father's shoulder and helped the blind old man to locate his bowl.

"You're right, I'm sure the Archduke will take some medicine and be all better. They have a cure for raging insanity now do they?" said the eldest man. "And then who'll we be left with? That crone that's who!" The old man continued to mutter, but with wilting strength.

"Is Archduke Choler really mad, dad?" asked the boy.

"Mad as they come!" piped the old man.

"Eat your soup, son. Father, you'll scare the boy."

"Never had a mental king as long as the Glenhavens were in," continued the eldest. Having reached the tender age where his opinion had become the most experienced, he wouldn't be stopped once he had started. "Now we have three tasters and the most beautiful cook in the city-"

"If you weren't blind Hamish, that would be quite the compliment," said Mrs Carnale, laying a hand on the folds of her glacial bosom.

"-and he'll only take food from his sister? Ridiculous!"

Jared stroked his son's wild hair as the boy slurped soup straight from the bowl.

"We're being paid and fed, Father. Many in the city dream of less."

"That doesn't mean we should take it. It would be half the insult if there had been a single attempt at poisoning in the last three hundred years, but there hasn't. At least, not one that the Cholers haven't plotted themselves," said the oldest man, spraying soup as he waved his spoon.

"Father, please-"

"Don't 'Father, please' me, Jared. I'm too old to be afraid. I don't think the gland works anymore," said the old man, folds of inelastic skin around his neck bobbing along to his tirade.

"Then fear for us. If one of his spies heard you, it would be the boy who would suffer."

"Yes, Hamish, eat your soup before it cools," said Mama Carnale.

The old man lowered his head closer to the bowl so he wouldn't spill.

The kitchens fell silent once more, except for the rattle and bubble of empty pans.

Chief Inspector Cawber ducked out of the kitchen's doorway. Beyond was a stone corridor, designed so the servants wouldn't have to be seen by the nobility. He found himself taking these narrow routes more and more often. The old man would have to be questioned; his conversation had been too close to treason. Maybe the boy too. He wondered if there was a spare cage in Brand Street for him. He rounded a corner, coming upon three young Constables. Steadfast's boys. One leant next to an ancient suit of armour, his boot on the wall. They talked and smoked their cigarettes. They didn't notice Cawber until he'd watched them a while.

When they saw him, they broke apart like startled minnows. They stood to attention, slivers of smoke rose from their hands, twisting like exotic dancers.

Cawber strode over to them, calculating the fear in each face. One of the boys' knees seemed ready to buckle, that or he desperately needed to pee. Silence stretched out, drawing sweat from the Constables' foreheads like snake venom. One of them blinked it out of his eyes, not daring to raise his hand to remove it.

"Do you have a spare one of those?" asked Cawber.

The Constables looked at each other.

"Well?"

Wavering hands reached for tobacco pouches. He was presented with three cigarettes. He took one.

"A light?"

A gas lighter *whomph*ed a tiny flame.

"Handy little things those," said Cawber, drawing the cigarette almost to its butt. "I think you boys get paid too much for what you don't do."

He blinked smoke from his eyes and decided he didn't want what remained of the cigarette. He pretended to look around for somewhere to put it, but held it out instead. The tallest Constable opened his hand. Cawber dropped the smoking butt into his palm.

"I expect letters of resignation from all three of you on Captain Steadfast's desk tomorrow morning," he said. "And I'll know if they're not there. But for now, you'll do your job. Get to your posts."

He continued down the corridor and, smiling to himself when he heard a yelp as the Constable finally dropped the smoking cigarette. Tugging aside one of the passageway's ancient tapestries produced a huff of dust, and Cawber was back into the servant's corridors again. Some substance had collected into a carpet on the ground, something like dust or mould, but the old gas lamps still flickered with memories of a time when the passageway was used regularly. Cawber stalked his way along it, certain that he'd meet no one coming the other direction. He passed several cupboards, none of which he'd ever decided to search. His curiosity was held exclusively for the innards of people rather than furniture. Passing a small alcove with a table and chair, he turned into an adjoining passage, much like the first, the walls made of wooden slats where coverings hadn't been deemed necessary. Coming to another tapestry, Cawber folded its edge with finger and thumb, and slid through.

The Archduke's office was much as it always had been in the few times he'd managed to peek inside while on guard duty. Only now there was no man-shaped bulge behind the curtains, no quivering slippers poking out from under the desk, and an unhealthy tidiness had come about the books and papers on every surface. To even an untrained eye, it had been made very clear that the Archduke was no longer in residence. Cawber held his breath. Above the high-backed chair, he could make out the piled grey mass that was Grinda Choler's hair; bobbing and swaying as she scribbled at her paperwork. Creeping forward, Cawber dipped inside his jacket, producing a thin steel blade designed specifically to not show its shape under this clothing. He could almost reach out and touch her now. Blade extended, he placed one hand on the chair's back for leverage.

"What have I told you about knocking?" asked Grinda.

Cawber quickly stepped up beside the chair as if it had been his intention all along, the tip of his knife picking under a fingernail. He found something there, and gouged it out; only a speck, and dark enough red that it could be mistaken for black. The crumb of blood landed on the paper beside Grinda's elbow. She snorted, shaking the paper. Her sneer burned his skin. Cawber circled the desk until he stood on the appropriate side.

"Apologies," he said. "I often find it useful to come and go in secret."

"Not with me. You'll approach the door like everyone else."

Cawber inclined his head in a shallow bow. Grinda's eyes returned to the desk top and she continued to write as she spoke.

"What news of Riccall?"

"A ghost, Lady Choler. My Inspectors have scoured the city for the rebel and his associates." Even Cawber averted his eyes when Grinda looked up at him.

"All except the part with him in, it seems. I'm starting to wonder if you're any more effective than Captain Steadfast after all."

Cawber fought back the snarl.

"The word is that he's gone into hiding," he lied.

Grinda looked at him, her eyes fixed on a point

somewhere inside his head. Cawber studied his toes. In the vacuum of speech, he found himself waffling.

"Left the city, that is. Altogether."

"No one leaves Greaveburn," said Grinda.

"It seems he thought otherwise, my Lady."

"So the scourge of Greaveburn just decides to leave. That sounds incredibly neat, Chief Inspector."

Cawber's eyes widened.

"I assure you, every investigation has been made, every person wrung until there was nothing left to question. Just like you ordered. He's left the Broken Folk to their own devices. Without their leader, they should be easy to-"

"I hear that the Brand Street cages are empty," interrupted Grinda from behind steepled fingers. Cawber didn't realise that he was squeezing the wrong end of his knife until a droplet of blood hit his boot.

"There've been no captures for a while. No riots. No rebels to catch. Without Riccall-"

Grinda held up a hand for silence. Leaning forward until her clasped hands rested on the desk, the ribs of her corset creaked against the wooden surface.

"Then I suggest you go into the Shackles and *find* some. And don't stop until every worthless peasant has been strung up. I gave you Brand Street for a reason. Use it."

The collar of Chief Inspector Cawber's shirt was slick with sweat, like an eel wrapped across his shoulders.

"Get out."

In his haste to leave, Cawber almost forgot to bow. Leaving a trail of blood, he let the door close behind him. Tugging a handkerchief from his back pocket, he applied it to his hand.

35

Riccall stood before a congregation of every Broken One in Greaveburn; a fallen Messiah. Clothed in dirt and rags, some swayed to counteract their physical shortcomings or were held upright by their companions. If it had been but two years before, Riccall would have withdrawn at the sight of them; a plague-pit come to life, all limb and twisted countenance. Now they were his family. His army.

"My friends!" he yelled, his voice travelling in swirls inside the warehouse's stark walls. "My friends, I am hungry. I see by your faces, by the united rumbling of your stomachs and by the skinny limbs of your children that you're hungry, too. We can't live this way, nor can we expect the Shackles to harbour us any more if this continues. My friends, action is needed."

He scanned the crowd. Children huddled here and there, or were raised on hunched shoulders. Few shared their parent's physical characteristics. Riccall knew that as time went on, as they grew, those children could become the face of the Broken Folk, their voice. Then they wouldn't need him and he would gratefully step aside in an age of acceptance and diplomacy. But for now, they had only conflict to exact their sway; only him to lead them.

There was a wary silence amongst the audience. Some turned to each other and a crescendo of mutters began to rise. Riccall cut it short, striving to control the noise:

"I come here to offer a solution, and the means to perform it. I believe we can feed not only ourselves but the Shackles as well. We can eat and replenish ourselves for the tasks ahead. We can watch our children grow and be well.

"Or we can starve. We can be cast out of the Shackles for the food it will bring to those who are left, lose our homes and most likely our lives. I would say this won't be easy, but I am aware of to whom I speak. You are a most singular people. You have seen adversity and have clung on despite it, and I know you can be even stronger. I've been beyond the walls, to Vale. I assure you, it's no myth. The banished have found each other beyond the reach of Greaveburn."

With that, an uncontrollable murmur rose from the crowd. Riccall shouted above it:

"I've seen the town that our brothers and sisters have built above the swamp. They fish and they farm a good life. They've made a home for themselves and we can be a part of it. We can leave now, as we are, and we can take nothing with us. But if we stay and fight our cause, Greaveburn can't ignore us. It doesn't understand us, but fears us. Would it not be better to leave for a new life in Vale, with a treaty for trade with the beast of Greaveburn in our grasp? Let's take its pride and weave our own from it.

"It can begin here. It can begin with the taking of food straight from their mouths. Let's show what we're made of. Let's show Greaveburn that if they deny us what we need, then we'll take it from them."

36

That he was denied assassination (as was the usual method of retirement in his occupation) was Loosestrife's final humiliation. Wheldrake was a coward, that was for certain. That his former assistant was simply humanitarian never crossed Loosestrife's mind. The notion was alien to him; pointless and frustrating.

With Wheldrake out of the lab, Loosestrife alternated between trying to loosen his restraint and indulging his imagination. To amuse himself, he pictured the grotesque tortures he would use to exact his revenge on his traitorous assistant. Only in the last six months had his imagination run out of bladed instruments.

A snigger crackled in his throat at the thought of a new felony to perform; something involving twisting, maybe the joint of a toe.

There was no denying that being in this situation had changed Loosestrife. His arrogance and appetite for carnage had fused like two rivers of lava; time and captivity had cooled it, and now his hatred was hard and black as obsidian. Where he'd been wary, but ultimately indifferent to Wheldrake's existence before, the full intensity of Loosestrife's wrath was now aimed his way.

That bar, that damn bar, locked by that damn Wheldrake. He scowled at it, called it further names under his breath. That bar was his nemesis. When he wished for a challenge to his intellect, he'd never dreamed that such a mundanely perfect answer would be given. It seemed that his intellect wasn't something that required testing. That wasn't the Gods' intention. They knew that his mind was unquestionable, even by Them. It was his resolve that was in question here.

Patience. Patience. There was a key to his freedom, and it was shaped like Patience.

Bloody, his palm slipped and slid across the bar's smug smoothness. He ignored the pain, barely wincing. Loosestrife's unyielding will leaked from him in briny droplets. The bar was shifting now, back and forth, back and forth like a pestle in a mortar. The stone was slowly wearing away. In a moment of frustration, Loosestrife tensed his feet against the wall and rattled the bar with all his tired might.

Breathless, he checked his handy work.

A crack.

A damned crack in the stone! It wasn't there before, he was sure.

Again, do it again.

Harder this time, he took to the bar.

The crack did nothing of interest.

With a lingering curse, he slumped against the wall and began to weep, his tears mingling with the sweat.

From behind him, soft as angel breath and twice as sweet, came the sound of falling stone.

37

Spears of light were thrown out into the night. A rising mist lapped at The Galleria's row upon row of windows. At the hub of civilised Greaveburn, on the Temple's gentle hill, the restaurant and wine house was nestled amongst ancient stone mansions and terraces.

Inside, safe from the chill and warmed by liquors of their choice, the high society of Greaveburn rubbed elbows. Women's tables were over by the windows, men's were by the bar, and neither mixed with the other. The Galleria wasn't a place for flirtation or social mingling. In Greaveburn's constantly rolling social climate, subordinate families attempted to align themselves with the upper ranks for protection and prestige. The Galleria ensured a haven from such bothersome pestering and from the crassness of the younger generation's mating rituals. Unless, of course, you knew where to look.

Corwater knew.

He sat in the inadequate light of the gas lamp across from Lord Happenstance, and watched.

"I wish you wouldn't insist on bringing me here,"

said the older gentleman.

"My Lord, this place is full of interest. Where else can you be likewise entertained?"

"I see nothing entertaining here, Corwater. Just a batch of high-nosed vultures."

"Really? Then let me share my amusement with you."

Corwater studied the rosy cheeked faces; starched collar and necktie, corset and bonnet. Eventually he found what he was looking for.

"Be discreet," he said. "But look at that young specimen by the window. Blue bonnet."

"What of her? A waif like any other."

"See how she tips a closed fan to her bosom, or what there is of it. Now look at the rather unfortunately-nosed fellow at the table there." Corwater tipped his cane slightly.

"I see him."

"They've been flirting all night," said Corwater with a smile.

"They haven't spoken to one another."

"And there's no need. The fan, you see, is to draw his attention to what she believes to be her best asset. Even mistakenly so. He's been watching her reflection in the window rather than looking directly at her. They've made eye contact that way at least three times. Now, if we wait-"

Corwater was cut short. The man with nostrils that could harbour Neanderthals made his excuses and got up from the table. He walked across the restaurant, past Corwater and Lord Happenstance in a cloud of lavender water, and made for the stairs. In short order, the young woman stood too.

"See? I didn't expect it so soon, but I knew it," said Corwater. He was almost giggling with delight.

"What am I seeing?" asked Happenstance.

"They're about to rendezvous. Upstairs. Both have made excuses to visit the bathroom, you can be sure of it."

"That's disgusting. They do this often?" asked Lord Happenstance. "This is normal practice amongst the young?"

"Oh believe me, they get plenty of practice, my Lord."

The young woman, no more than a girl in truth, drifted past them and made for the foot of the stairs. She searched the room for observers before mounting the bottom step.

Corwater caught her eye.

With his cane pressed to his mouth, he gave the girl a wink. Her face flushed like a beet and she lifted her skirts to swiftly ascend. He laughed aloud. Others in the room cast their eyes his way and received a cheery wave in return.

"This generation are animals," said Lord Happenstance.

"Animals?" said Corwater. "Not at all, not at all. They're exercising their urges as any human being does. Albeit in a roundabout way. Are you telling me that you've never ... partaken outside of wedlock?"

"As you well know, I've never married, but I do the proper thing and don't cavort with ladies." Happenstance lowered his voice, hoping that Corwater would follow his lead.

"I see. You reserve your *cavorting* for ... professional women?"

Lord Happenstance adjusted his collar and straightened his waistcoat. Before speaking he took a large taste of his brandy.

"I think this conversation is over."

"And I'll oblige, but let me leave you with this. I maintain that the only difference between ladies and professional lovers is that the latter accept what they are, the former simply enjoy it."

It was at that point, as if to accent the end of a painful conversation, that the screaming started.

A hundred heads turned toward the windows, the night outside making it hard to see. People squinted, craned and pressed their faces closer to the glass.

A young girl screamed, and in her haste to get away from whatever she'd seen, went sprawling, her hooped skirts flying like peacock feathers.

"Whoops, one too many, my dear?" chuckled Corwater. But it died in his throat when another scream came from the fallen girl's friend. His face fell.

An exodus of the elite began like the swarming of swallows. Scraping tables and clattering chairs rose to ear-battering heights. Everyone was moving away from the windows.

"What the hell is going on?" asked Lord Happenstance.

The companions fought their way against the surge of people. Some were jostled violently aside, others knocked to the ground. Yelps from some of the women could be heard amongst the din. As he reached the window, Lord Happenstance found the girl who had fallen first, her skirts ripped and face bruised by the trampling of her friends. He lifted her to her feet.

Whimpering, she wriggled from Happenstance's hand and scuttled across the restaurant, clutching her damaged skirts to her, leaving them alone.

"What *is* that?" he heard Corwater ask.

Sections of the mist rose like swell, forming into individual shapes with the fog rolling from them like sea foam. Lamplight from The Galleria's tall windows stopped just short of where the figures crowded in frustrating darkness. Corwater pressed his face closer to the glass, strained his eyes, but saw nothing he recognized as human.

As one, the shapes surged. Lurching toward The Galleria, they looked like animate puppets made of rag and mismatched toy parts.

As the creatures reached the glass, and the darkness finally rolled back, more screams rang out.

With Corwater and Happenstance stood on the inside, dark swaying shapes without, a standoff seemed in progress.

Instead, Corwater lifted the window's latch, and the doors were thrown open.

"What's he doing?" yelled a rotund fellow wearing a smaller waistcoat than was decent for his size. "Leave them closed you fool!"

Corwater and Happenstance each stepped aside to allow the insurgents entry.

"Stand down, idiot. They're not here for you," said Happenstance with a glance like lead.

The Broken Folk made straight for the kitchens. A chain was formed. Bread, cheese and meat drifted away into the night. The rotund man made a grab for a bottle of wine as it went past, but missed.

Corwater's eye was caught by a tall figure in the dark outside. At first glance it could have been a statue, or part of the beards of lichen which coated the square's disused fountain. But he could feel the man's gaze upon him sure as he would feel the Devil's.

"That is a dangerous man," he muttered.

"The Guard are coming!" someone shouted, cheering for the cavalry.

The Broken Folk bolted, causing destruction as they fled into the street, their arms laden with food. The fat man approached Corwater and prodded at his abdomen, the only part he could reach.

"You let them in. They stole our food!" blustered the blowhard.

Corwater regarded the man as he would something flea-ridden. With deliberate disgust, he pressed the tip of his cane on the man's barrel chest and moved him away.

"We started it," he said.

The guard filtered into the square from every side street and alleyway, panting, with swords drawn.

Steadfast stood amongst them, Cawber at his elbow. Only the Chief Inspector's face and silver badge stood out from the dark.

"Looks like we don't have to round up the Broken Folk," said Cawber. "I told you, didn't I? Starve them out. This is our lucky night, Steadfast."

Steadfast's skin crawled. His hand strayed to the copper shield on his own uniform.

"*Yours,* you mean. This will keep you in blood for a month."

"Only if your boys catch them. They don't seem to be doing much at the minute," sneered Cawber. "I'll leave you to it. Just send them my way when you're done playing with them."

Cawber walked away, the gleam of moonlight on his badge disappearing into the dark.

"Stop them, then!" Steadfast yelled, shaking the nearest Constable.

"But sir," quivered the young man. "We're not trained to fight monsters!"

Steadfast regarded the sweaty young man, and the lad's fear cooled him like hot iron dipped in water. "They're not monsters, Constable. They're just people. Now get in there and arrest them!"

Riccall's army were fighting back, and losing. Some were hauled into the air by the guards, kicking and thrashing, wailing with fear and frustration; others were brought crashing to the ground. Food rolled between the bodies. Fruit burst on the cobbles, their juices mingled with blood and sweat.

The Broken Folk were too hungry, too tired, or too sick to fight back. Where the stronger resisted, blood pooled on the cobbles.

Joseph ran through the throng, ducking weapons and fists. A young girl sprawled across the floor in front of him, a guard grasping at her legs as she tried to escape. Joseph kicked the guard hard in the face, sending him rolling, and dragged the girl to her feet.

He ran on, shoving the girl in front of him, making his way back to the fountain, and to Riccall.

From beside the fountain, Riccall stood with a slack jaw.

Joseph shook him by the arm.

"Riccall, help them. They're dying!"

There was no answer.

"Riccall!"

Nothing.

Joseph shoved Riccall one last time. Cursing, he ran back into the mob of panicked bodies and screams.

Riccall watched him go.

He blinked.

Blinked again.

"Run," he whispered. Then, louder, "To the sewers! Run! *Run!*"

From where Steadfast stood, he could see the hooded figure in profile. When it began to shout, he drew his sword to advance. That man had to be Riccall. He hadn't left at all, it seemed, just bided his time. Who else would dare lead the Broken Folk on a raid of the inner city?

"You there! Stop!" he yelled, and ran forward, but skidded to a halt meters from his quarry.

Riccall turned to meet him.

The sounds of slaughter surrounded Riccall. Tears streamed down his face. Through blurry eyes, he turned to meet the guard that advanced on him, and froze. Wiping his face with a threadbare sleeve, he recognised his adversary.

Steadfast.

The Broken Folk, or what were left of them, were escaping. In their haste, someone shoved Riccall so hard that he stumbled.

His hood was knocked loose. Finally, Steadfast would know the face of Greaveburn's scourge.

"Stand up. Stand up and face me you coward," he muttered.

The cloaked figure collected itself, rose from its knee.

Riccall's face was sallow in the moonlight.

"*No.*"

Darrant had aged quickly. Lines scored his forehead, a deep scar pulled at his left eye and puckered the cheek, drawing his lip into a permanent grimace.

A sensation of surrealism came upon Steadfast. There was nothing to tell between this moment and the frequent nightmares he suffered. Was he asleep? Or were his dreams now so powerful as to be made material in the waking world?

Like the curdling of milk, Riccall watched Steadfast's anger turn to anguish.

He hadn't been forgotten, it seemed.

"This isn't the time," Riccall muttered, and turned toward the sewer cover.

"Darrant!" Steadfast yelled, but got no answer.

Once more, Riccall fell into the sewer, and was gone.

Steadfast didn't give chase. He stood for a long while before his mind finally closed off. If allowed, he could stand on that spot and whittle over his encounter with Darrant for the rest of his life. But he had to move. Now.

The mist had been dispersed by the riot. All that were left were guards, pressing the struggling and wailing Broken Folk to the ground, and the corpses of the fallen.

The nobles, feeling that the battle was safely over, had spilled out into the street to watch.

"What are you looking at?" sneered Steadfast. Advancing on the bejewelled leeches, his anger broke. *"What the hell are you staring at?"*

Recoiling as if struck, the nobility jostled their way back inside and the doors of the Galleria were slammed closed. Only two men remained; one an older gentlemen in a grey-blue suit, the other a sleek youngster with sensual eyes. Steadfast paid them little attention. There would still be much work to do tonight, work that could only darken his soul further.

Riccall crumpled on the sewer walkway.

From the ground, he grasped out, catching a pair of legs that ran past.

"Joseph, where's Joseph?" he implored to the weeping face of Nessa, a girl who's hands had been taken by disease at birth. In the crook of her arm she held a loaf of bread that she guarded fiercely.

"Let me go, let me *go*." Nessa struggled but Riccall held fast, almost dragging her to the ground with him.

"Where *is* he?"

"Gone. He's gone. Let me go."

Riccall clung to her for a moment. She stopped her struggling when he began to weep.

"Please," she said. "I just want to go home."

She slid from his grip and jogged away into the sewer, leaving him alone.

Riccall stumbled across the planks that lead to Rickety Bridge's main platform, his finger-shy hand tight on the rope banister.

Others had already been this way.

Some still huddled in the jumble; faces peered out from between furniture and bric-a-brac like forgotten toys. Birgit swept between them with rags and water, cleansing and binding wounds where she could. She puffed at her hair, which was obviously in her way, but she still wouldn't tie it back from her face.

Mrs Foible didn't look at him as he approached. He was glad. In his state, he wasn't sure he could take the power of her eyes.

"Riccall!" It was Narelle, safe in her bunk. But Riccall didn't answer.

It took Birgit barring his way to make him stop.

"What have you done?" she asked in a whisper. Her eyes were shimmering with tears. "What have you *done*?"

He didn't answer; couldn't.

"Where's Joseph?" Birgit pressed. She shook him by the fold of his shirt. "Where *is* he?"

"Gone," Riccall managed, and that was all.

Birgit's strike came fast, its intent, more than the physical force, burning into Riccall's face. It came again, and again, knocking saliva from Riccall's mouth before Chintz moved between them. Behind her, Narelle's cherubic features were tight, her tears held back by clenched teeth. Chintz held Birgit in one arm, folding her into him, and pushed lightly with his other immense hand at Riccall's chest.

He wasn't wanted here. This was no longer his home.

Birgit turned on Mrs Foible, screaming through Chintz's embrace.

"You! Why didn't you stop him? You could have stopped him!"

Riccall left against a backdrop of sobs, moans of pain and anguish that he had caused. About to round the corner, he felt the sting of air, and a clatter came from the stone walkway behind him.

It was his sword.

Birgit screamed something at him before Chintz could take her away from the wooden railing. He didn't hear it, but he got the point.

He looked once more to Mrs Foible. This time he wanted her to see him, to recognise him for what he was and what she'd failed to see in him before. But she didn't.

He snatched up the sword and saw Rickety Bridge for the last time. Unable to return above, and no longer welcome below, Riccall retreated to the ancient darkness beneath Greaveburn.

38

hole sections of road were diverted around the construction teams. Two streets away, where New Common Road met the main causeway, Steadfast spotted a cattle drive merging with the other traffic. He called to his men across the junction, his voice lost in the smothering din of the street. In the end, he had to use his whistle to get their attention. He motioned wildly in semaphore, and shouted again.

"Stop those cattle! Send them elsewhere. No, I don't care where. There's no room for them here!"

It was a natural reaction, even for the nobility. They had demanded that the Archduke seal the sewers in the inner city. Grinda Choler had passed Steadfast the orders. The Archduke was indisposed, she had said. The writing on the letter, when he eventually opened it, was almost illegible. There was little to mark it as the Archduke's, or even as that of an adult. Grinda had explained what it said with much more detail than could be contained in the few lines of scrawl.

A hundred stonemasons worked through the night to create the rough stone discs, and since first light every spare man had begun blocking sewer covers. Anyone without a crane or a good score of men would find them impossible to move. Still, the blockages caused havoc with the market day traffic. Steadfast had been diverting carts and carriages with his men since the night before. By sunrise, everyone should have been at their destinations, filling stalls and serving produce. It was now midday and the gridlock was impenetrable.

Knowing that Darrant lay coiled somewhere beneath his feet finally justified Steadfast's paranoia. In the strangest way, he felt better. His guilt for killing Darrant had been lifted and old, familiar fear remained. Fear was something he could handle.

Yelling at a nearby Sergeant to take over, Steadfast stepped down from his post and was lost in the crowd.

In an effort to make Wheldrake wait, Steadfast had decided to walk the long way back to the guard house. With the masses of irate merchants and public, he was slowed even further. He barely had to walk, as the swell of the crowd moved him with its tides. Everywhere faces contorted into grimaces. He passed through an open area where an impromptu market had risen.

He strode up to two of the nearest merchants, one a rotund fellow with a potbelly to rest a pint glass on, the other a string bean with a thin moustache.

"What's going on here?" he demanded.

"We're setting up shop," said Potbelly.

"You can't start a market in the street," said Steadfast. "When the traffic gets moving again, you'll have to pack it all up."

"This lot isn't going to get moving again, today," said Stringbean, jabbing his thumb toward the crowd.

"There are steps in place to get the traffic moving-" started Steadfast.

"It's not steps we need, Captain, it's more flamin' roads!" said Potbelly.

They both turned back to distributing their wares, shouts rising like battle cries.

Steadfast skulked away, elbowing his way into the crowd. In a moment he had been turned around so many times that he'd lost his bearings. A small troop of pigs were driven past by a young boy with a stick. He headed for a row of houses nearby, not bothering to apologise when he stood on folk to get through.

Ducking into Grape Alley, panting, he diverted sweat from brow to sleeve.

"There's no way I'm going back out there," he said, and took the alley instead.

Despite his diversion, Steadfast reached the guard house and still had time to read three reports before Wheldrake arrived.

Down the narrow stairs, the bustle of the guard house had risen to a clamour of worried voices. Reports of Broken Folk walking the streets were coming from all over the city. Almost all turned out to be overreactions to the usual oddments that walked Greaveburn's streets day to day by irate gentlemen and ladies. Darrant had managed to cause mass panic so easily.

"We have to stop him," Steadfast said. "He's mad."

"Well, if anyone has cause-" said Wheldrake.

"Don't."

"What?"

"Just don't."

Wheldrake stalked between the piles of Riccall reports, occasionally fingering a page or two.

"You should really do something with these," he said. "Or at least have someone dispose of them for you."

"Darrant," said Steadfast. "We were talking about Darrant."

"Yes. We were," said Wheldrake. "If you'd said the same thing a week ago, I would have called it an extension of your guilt-fuelled paranoia. Which, may I say, was becoming tiresome. Now, I think I might owe you an apology."

"Go on then." Steadfast sat back in his chair, hands spread out on the desk.

"That was it," said Wheldrake, not bothering to turn. "Now, I think I need to ask you this, because the outcome will no doubt ride on it. What is your motivation, Captain?"

"Motivation? What are you getting at, Wheldrake? I know who Riccall is now. I know *where* he is. And he's growing bolder. For the sake of Greaveburn, he must be stopped before anarchy tears us apart."

Wheldrake perched himself on a spare corner of Steadfast's desk and stared out of the window. A sense of foreboding tickled his guts.

"That's noble," he said. "I'm glad it has nothing to do with your fear of reprisals. It wouldn't end well if you were motivated to stop Darrant. Or should we call him Riccall now? Simply so that he wouldn't get to you first. It seems to me that it would be easy to fall into that trap, don't you agree?"

Steadfast remained silent, but glared at the scientist, his face puckered into anger.

"Are you going to help me or not?"

"I'm not entirely sure what you expect me to do," said Wheldrake, setting his golden brown gaze on the Captain.

"Neither am I. Yet. But when I know, so will you."

39

Through the tunnel toward the laboratory, Wheldrake stalked with sure footsteps despite the pitch darkness. He turned the corner without needing to see it and walked out onto the steel platform that had once been an entrance for the late General Leager.

The laboratory was in darkness.

Damn it.

He stormed down the platform, headed for the fuse room. It had been only a week since he'd changed the enormous fuses that kept the eel's power in check. Despite his uncanny strength, his shoulder still ached from lifting them into place. They couldn't have blown, but they had.

Mildew-filtered light provided a green glow to navigate by. In that half-light, Wheldrake's eyes were tricked time and again into forming shapes that weren't there, dangers where there were none. He swore to remove some of Loosestrife's machinery soon, to strip it down and be done with it. He was sickened by looking at macabre fancies of that brilliantly deranged mind.

He made it to the alcove that was Professor Loosestrife's prison. Fumbling to light the oil lamp on his desk, he whispered without knowing why:

"Professor?"

Nothing.

"Professor?"

Silence.

Stamping across to the alcove, he lifted the lamp high.

"What happened to the damn *lights*?"

The lamp's meagre flicker was barely enough to illuminate the alcove's emptiness. The bars which had held the Professor captive lay on the floor surrounded by chunks of perished stone.

Wheldrake shuddered.

Fear reached his throat and tightened its fist.

Loosestrife rose like bile behind Wheldrake, placing a hand on his assistant's narrow shoulder. Amber lamplight squirmed over his face like enraged insects.

Wheldrake could smell him now, the musk of ancient sweat.

When Loosestrife hissed, it was so close that Wheldrake felt the spittle on his ear.

"Why, I turned them off."

Wheldrake tried to spin, to catch the Professor off-guard, but the blow had already come. The metal of the Professor's hand pummelled Wheldrake's neck, knocking him to the ground with a grunt.

"Coward," spat Loosestrife. "Petty, worthless, coward."

The kick rolled Wheldrake into the alcove.

"Can you smell it?" Loosestrife sneered. "That is the stench of the pit in your nostrils. It's rising up to claim you, boy. Can you smell it?"

As Loosestrife's hand whistled down, Wheldrake exploded upward, fists engaged. They collided like freight trains, pissing steam and screaming like twisted metal.

Falling back into the laboratory's shadows together, only the sounds of their hellish struggle identified them. A shriek of agony from Wheldrake echoed between the laboratory's walls before escaping out into the street above.

An elderly couple huddled under their parasol. The air was so crystal clear that the sunlight stung their eyes. They stepped gingerly over a grate, not wanting to stumble.

A fiendish yell, as if rising from Hell itself, issued from the vent.

The couple stared, frozen in disbelief, and scurried on, holding each other up.

Wheldrake fell against the metal door, bloody and panting. Reaching upward, he span the locking wheel and fell inside. The blistering light of the eel's sanctum assaulted his eyes. Screwing them shut, he braced himself against the door as Loosestrife pounded on the other side.

"Coward! Craven, spineless, whelp!"

With each word, the Professor hammered at the steel door, making craters in the metal with his artificial hand. He wrenched at the locking wheel, twisting it into a pretzel before it snapped free.

Wheldrake could taste blood.

The Professor's hammering echoed around the eel's room and pounded at his ears. A thousand questions ran through his mind, and not one answer.

He fell back when the door was yanked open. Loosestrife stood over him, scowling. Wheldrake threw himself to the side, Loosestrife's boot missing his head by sheer luck alone.

He was about to die. The Professor was in an unstoppable rage. Nothing but Wheldrake's death would end this now.

Watching the maggot squirm away, Loosestrife gave himself a moment to smile. He took his goggles from their place on the wall and slid them on. With the room's light diminished, he could enjoy Wheldrake's demise all the better.

He followed Wheldrake slowly, kicking at his ribs or knocking his arms from beneath him as he tried to escape.

"You are pathetic," he jeered, as Wheldrake fell against the central dais. The assistant's hands scraped against the plinth in an effort to raise himself.

Finally on his feet, Wheldrake turned to his master. The plinth held him upright where his legs had all but given up. He wrapped a bloody arm about himself, feeling so ragged that, if he let go, he was sure his body would topple into its constituent parts; a pile of agonised Wheldrake on the floor.

He fumbled amongst the cell components on the dais, finally wrapping his aching fingers around a heavy bearing.

Loosestrife ducked unnecessarily. Wheldrake's aim had been bad.

The cell behind the Professor exploded, shards of glass peppering his back as the hurled bearing missed its mark. The eel flopped to the ground to squirm against his boots. A stream of electricity lashed outward to earth itself on the dais behind Wheldrake. The assistant shielded his eyes from the flash.

"Enough now," said Loosestrife, adjusting his goggles. "I've had enough of you. Lay down and die quickly. I can't be bothered to kill you slow."

Through his light-scarred eyes, Wheldrake didn't see Loosestrife until the Professor was on him. Loosestrife lunged, cuffing Wheldrake so hard that he stumbled to the wall.

Wheldrake's eyes focused on the cell before him. Blood stung his eye where it had trickled down his face. There was so much pain that his brain had stopped registering half of it. The eel thrashed in its prison.

Pressing his eyes closed, Wheldrake forced more tears to flush out the blood. His ears twitched. Behind him the Professor was taking no time to tiptoe. With tears and blood mingling like oil and water on his cheeks, Wheldrake opened his eyes, and was ready.

Air whistled through the bars of Loosestrife's artificial hand as it came down.

Wheldrake threw himself to the side.

The battery cell exploded as Loosestrife's crashed through the glass. Wheldrake span clumsily, his battered hands finding the thin material of Loosestrife's shirt. He shoved, and the Professor fell head first into the cell as it released its charge.

Wheldrake was thrown away, arms over his face.

Loosestrife whirled around, electricity caressing his body in a glowing net of energy. His hair was a mane of flames that gave off embers in a spiralling cloud. The pain was everywhere; it was his body and the air and the light.

Wheldrake fought for breath.

The Professor reeled about the room to the crackle of fire and spit of boiling flesh. Where he fell, more cells were shattered by his thrashing arms until the ground was a mass of squirming and glass. Electricity crackled in a subterranean storm, dancing on the dais and crawling across the walls in sheets of deadly lightning.

There was too much power let loose to stop it now, even if Wheldrake reached the great switches beyond the maelstrom of light and fire and silent hurt. The laboratory was done for, and so was he if he didn't move fast.

Fingers clenched against the floor's grating, Wheldrake dragged himself over the eel room's threshold and into the laboratory. Wheldrake drew a shivering breath and pressed his cheek against the cool steel floor. The air smelled of cooking fish and flesh.

Something in the battery room exploded. Fire belched out of the doorway, eager to taste Wheldrake's skin. He felt the heat of it through his clothes, so hot that he rolled onto his back, certain that he was on fire. He wasn't, but he soon would be. There was oil, and paper, and innumerable flammables about the laboratory that would spell his death if they were to catch alight.

Up, up. You must get up.

First, Wheldrake rose to his hands, elbows shuddering with the weight of his own body, and crawled forward. Grabbing for a stool, he used it to reach his feet.

The thought crossed his mind to close the battery room door, and slow the fire's spread. But, as he reached out to it, his hand began to crinkle like paper with the heat of the metal. It was no good, there was only retreat.

Stumbling through the stifling blanket of smoke, he pressed a sleeve across his face. His thoughts turned to the Professor, and the blaze that engulfed him.

So quiet. Loosestrife hadn't made a sound.

Wheldrake had the vile sensation that his master could still emerge from the smoke at any moment, a vengeful angel wrapped in flame. But no, he was surely dead now. His evil was over.

Another explosion knocked Wheldrake to the ground with the force of blasted air. His ears rang. Gouts of flame blossomed from beneath the floor. The fire had spread downward then, to the other levels. The glass apparatus used to formulate the elixir on the level below was filled with any number of odd chemicals. Only the Gods and Loosestrife knew what else was on the floors below that. Loosestrife had always kept them locked, and Wheldrake had never had the stomach to develop that level of curiosity.

All of this he thought whilst crawling toward his only chance for escape. Through choking clouds, Wheldrake could see nothing, but he knew the chute's hatch when his hand finally found it. Its latch was still cool as he yanked it open, and the gust of chill air it exuded, although tinged with the scent of distant sewage, Wheldrake welcomed.

Hauling himself up, he slid into the darkness, away from the fire above, through stone and mould and slime, into the bowels of Greaveburn.

40

"There are vents and sewer covers from the broken spire to the Academe billowing with smoke," said Steadfast. "They're working hard, but still have no idea where the fire is coming from."

Grinda Choler sat behind the Archduke's desk.

It seemed of late that more and more time was being spent dealing with these crises than on running the city. Greaveburn ground to a halt every few days as the population were drafted to deal with the latest stream of emergencies. First the riots, then building the pipelines to stop The Ague, then the Broken Folk's invasion, and now a fire somewhere beneath the streets.

Grinda knew that as she spoke to the Captain, Legat lay foetal somewhere. It had been two days since she'd seen him; her last visit disturbed her more than she cared to admit. In a rare moment of lucidity, Legat had stood at the window to his apartment in his night gown, looking out over a city that had briefly been his.

The pillar of smoke rising from Hanker Street held the Archduke rapt, his rheumy eyes reflecting the smouldering skyline. Then he'd started to sob, so deep and heavy that Grinda almost expected him to stop breathing. She had caught him as his knees gave way. Both splayed on the floor, his head in her lap, tears collected like mercury drops on her ebony dress.

Back in the office, she was once again composed, but couldn't ignore Legat's words.

Burning from the roots. Burning us out.

This fire from below was an act of revenge from the Broken Folk, of that there was no mistake. While their captured minions swung in the Brand Street cages, they plotted to take Greaveburn from the foundations, even if it meant bringing it down on their heads.

Be careful on whom you tread, one day those same people will form the very ground beneath your feet. If she could remember who had said that, she would have them hanged for smugness.

"This is an intolerable standoff," she said, shoving thoughts of her sobbing brother to the back of her mind until her visit later that day. "The mutants think they can hold us to ransom from the relative safety of their sewers and slums. So far, I have-"

She looked up at Steadfast, but saw no flicker.

"-the Archduke has been lenient. It is time we ended this for good and take back the city. We are all living in fear, and are tired of it."

"Let me have them, Ma'am. I'll take a troop of our finest, hunt them through the sewers and be rid of them, and Riccall-"

"No," Grinda interrupted. "No, you won't. Because you're incompetent. The problem, Captain Steadfast, is that we are trying to fight honourably-"

Once more, not a flicker on Steadfast's face.

"-against a dishonourable foe. There are men, I believe, who would provide services more efficient than your own, although distasteful. Perhaps, however, the time has come for distaste. Your job, Captain, will be to find these men and grant them the powers necessary to rid us of the Broken Folk once and for all. I expect immediate results."

Steadfast said nothing, but saluted and left the office.

Barghest snapped to attention as he exited.

"Did you hear any of that, Sergeant?" he asked.

"Not a word, sir."

"Good."

"Good luck, sir."

"Thank you, Sergeant."

The focus of the fire-fighting efforts took place on Hanker Street, a wide carriageway that passed by Loosestrife's old place and, further down, the Academe. One of Wheldrake's pipes ran down its centre, a pump every two hundred yards. Hoses led from each pump, shoved down into the tiny drainage grates by the side of the road. There had been no time to remove the great stone blocks from the larger sewer covers themselves. Steadfast stood beside one of those blocks, watching soot-covered Greaveburners scamper up and down the wooden steps which straddled the water pipes, taking turns at the pumps. Those stone blocks had been such a good idea at the time. But every step forward was a step back.

The smoke was clearing, only to be replaced by steam which was no better. Wherever the fire was coming from, they had doused it by sheer luck. There was no telling how deep some of the oldest sewers went, or what was down there. But by the amount of steam, something very hot beneath the streets was being cooled.

The fire could have been intentional or not, but Steadfast wasn't going to be the one to tell Grinda Choler that.

There was still much work to do here, and plenty of busybodies to do it, and so he began the long walk back to the guard house. He would have to change if he were to enter the Shackles and stay alive. No one could be allowed to recognise him, and he was certain they wouldn't once he was out of uniform. The helmet, royal blue jacket and shiny buttons made him Captain of the Guard; without it he was unmemorable.

An end to the Broken Folk. That meant an end to Darrant.

For once, the Cholers and Steadfast had a mutual agenda. His regret for murdering Darrant was seeping away. If he had done his task properly; if he'd shown no mercy to his friend, then Darrant wouldn't be seeking to crush the city for the sake of the mutants.

For once, Steadfast had the bigger picture in mind and, beneath the dust of centuries, that picture was Greaveburn.

41

The tornado of ravens cawed and croaked in an attempt to call swift death to Brand Street. Broken Folk moaned and cried from their cages.

A pair of guards wandered past at a steady pace. Seeing one of the Broken Folk had fallen asleep, a guard rattled the bars with his sword, laughing at the startled prisoner with the bloodied face.

Riccall flinched.

From his alley, he watched the guards stroll away, content in their conversation. He'd watched them five times now; they wouldn't be back for ten minutes or more.

Striding out of the darkness and across the avenue, he made for Joseph's cage.

"Joseph," he whispered, knowing that his friend was alive only because the ravens were leaving him alone.

Joseph's face was a lumpy mess on one side, and purple right down the neck. No doubt there would be more bruises beneath his clothes. Clotted blood matted in his hair and eyelashes. A single dirtied foot dangled from between the bars. When he spoke, it was muffled by his swollen gums:

"You came *cfgh*." Joseph's twitch caused him such agony now that he whimpered.

"Yes," said Riccall, checking the street.

"Good."

"Joseph, I'm sorry."

Riccall's friend simply nodded, squinting through his swollen eyes with no hint of hatred.

"Don't just nod, Joseph. Tell me. Blame me and curse me. I deserve it." Riccall reached up and grasped the cage's bars, lifting himself to better receive his punishment.

"Not your *cfgh* fault, Riccall," managed Joseph, although the name was mangled by the slur. "You did *cfgh*...you did what you thought best."

"That's just it," said Riccall, tears streaking the dirt on his cheeks. He cried so often now, and so readily. "I did what I knew was wrong. I took revenge and used you all to do it. I led you here and left you, Joseph. You should despise me."

"A good *cfgh* man." Sliding down in his cage, Joseph gripped Riccall's sleeve.

"No!" Riccall pulled away.

Down the street, the ravens had begun to feed. They hammered at a cage, slipping between the bars with their bloodied talons and rending beaks. There was only meat in that cage now, thought Riccall, only meat.

Pressing his hand to his mouth, he turned away.

The guards would be back soon. He was tempted to let them find him here. He had his sword now, if he gave fight maybe they would kill him, and all of his captured friends would feel some justice had been done.

"Riccall."

Joseph was trying to call him, but couldn't raise his voice.

"Yes?"

"Go," said Joseph as if reading his mind.

Slipping a hand inside his cloak, Riccall produced a loaf. He passed it up to Joseph and made to leave.

"Thank you, Joseph. You're a better man than me."

Joseph watched Riccall slip back into the Shackles, knowing that nothing he could have said would have tortured his friend more than his own guilt.

Returning to his slow death, he noticed the little girl in the next cage. Her stare was crystal blue. He tried to smile despite the pain and produced a grimace.

"Sleep," he managed, nodding assurances. "Be better *cfgh* tomorrow."

The dirty little girl settled down into the lap of her mother, who was slowly growing cold.

42

He was a little out of breath because Temple Hill was steepest here, but Corwater still managed to whistle. Quickly checking the road, he stepped down from the curb and started to cross. Two hackney carriages rumbled by. He darted between them, dodging manure, and up onto the opposite pavement.

Before going so far as the Galleria, his boots clacked on the stone steps that led to the upper terrace.

He met other nobles coming and going in their relaxed strides. Up here the rich were safe from the sufferings of lower Greaveburn, the pillar of smoke was captured by the wind and whipped into a mere curiosity miles away, the tower of swirling ravens, even further. An uprising of rebellious Broken Folk was nothing but an article in the newspaper, read and quickly forgotten. Bad things were happening to other people, far away, and that was the way they liked the world to work.

Corwater swam in their ignorance like a velvet water snake. He traded greetings as if he was happy to do so. His days were a constant masquerade of grudging politeness. Except for Happenstance, of course.

Trailing his fingers along the stone balustrade, he stopped to gaze down into the street, but only briefly. There was feigning nonchalance, and then there was denying yourself a pleasure. Corwater was eager to reach his friend's home. His visit would be an eventful one today. Today, he had news.

Entering without knocking, Corwater laid his coat across the elderly butler's knee. The servant had fallen asleep propped in the corner by the door. Corwater kept the cane with him; it occupied his hands.

It was too early for Happenstance to be breakfasting, and so Corwater took a high-backed chair in the lounge, first turning it so he could see into the hall. A maid, who was used to his impromptu visits, set down a cup of steaming tea by his elbow. When he realised she was still stood there, he rewarded her with a sideways flicker of his eyebrows that sent her scuttling away with red cheeks.

Just as he was deliberating how much of a waste it was, another girl came down the stairs. She was new to him and, by the look of her, new to the profession as well. Happenstance was a kind soul, if not a little lonely, and always paid the girls handsomely for their time. She was well bathed, her hair still wet and clinging to her slender neck in brunette curlicues. She wore a simple white dress, the kind Happenstance always gave to these visitors of his. Her other dress would be washed and fixed by the staff and she would receive it through the tradesman's entrance at a later date.

She drifted down the staircase, the shimmer of girlhood gone from her eyes. Fingers like lily petals tested her face for tears that hadn't come yet. She struck Corwater with something that he hadn't felt in a long time. It wasn't pity, or sympathy, but it made his heart heavy. He almost didn't recognise it.

Stood at the foot of the stairs, eyes cast down, she fumbled in the pocket of her new dress, no doubt with the other offering Happenstance had given her, as if wondering its worth beside what she had given away.

It isn't enough, thought Corwater, shocking himself. *It could never be enough.*

She looked up, as if feeling Corwater's eyes on her. Her face flushed a tantalizing pink. Bundling her dress' skirts off the ground, she bolted like a startled deer toward the front door. Corwater hauled himself out of the chair. The girl made a little whimper as she heard his boots hurry across the floor; another noble with an appetite for servant girls, right behind her.

Before she reached the door, Corwater took her elbow. She felt soft leather against her palm; could smell its heavy tang. She daren't look down for fear of what was about to happen.

"Spend it well, my dear," he said. "Spend it for something good. Make something of it so that you never have to return."

The door opened and she ran out into the daylight, almost colliding with a pair of ladies in her haste. She swerved past them without stopping, and ran along the terrace, taking the stairs to the street two at a time until she was out of sight.

"Good morning." Happenstance was coming down the stairs, adjusting his necktie. "Corwater? I said, 'good morning'"

"Yes, I know."

"What's the matter with you?" the Lord asked, peeking out of the open door and seeing nothing of interest.

"Nothing. Just taking some air," said Corwater. "If we're to have dinner, I'm afraid it's on you. I appear to have left my wallet at home."

The meal had been good as always, but Corwater had barely tasted it.

"A house in Ginnal Avenue began to leak water out into the street. They say the sewers backed up with such force that there was water at the windows. The Gods know why it decided to leak out there."

Happenstance gave nods and sounds of agreement, commenting little.

Corwater was so tempted to just tell him the *real* news in an effort to knock some interest out of his friend, but he must wait. Patience was a virtue, and he didn't have many others.

"The fire is finally out, they think, although there is still no idea where it came from. They say the water might take months to drain away before anyone can get down there to take a look."

"Do they still think the Broken Folk did it?" asked Happenstance.

"Yes. But they're blaming a dose of influenza, the waxing moon and an inflation in cabbage prices on the Broken Folk, too."

"Point well made."

Corwater leaned in close, beckoning Happenstance to do the same.

"And now, are you ready for the most delicious news you will ever hear?"

"You certainly have me intrigued, if that was your intention."

"Come here then, lean in," said Corwater, exasperated at his companion's lack of enthusiasm.

"Your theatrics are bothersome," said Happenstance, but leant in all the same.

"Legat Choler...is dead."

"WHAT?!"

"*Shush!*"

Corwater flapped his hands for calm, searching the room for observers. This uncharacteristic secrecy startled Happenstance almost as much as the news itself.

"They found him yesterday, by the smell. He'd

lifted the floorboards in his quarters and crawled in to hide from the Broken Folk. They say the last thing he said was that they were trying to burn him out."

"Who is this 'They' of whom you constantly speak? How do you get such information before any of the rest of us? You're a bafflement, Corwater."

"Never mind where I heard it, I just did, and it's true. He's dead and Old Crone Choler is taking over. Or rather, she's taking over *officially*. They'll announce it tomorrow."

43

Shhhrink
    Shhhhhhhrrrrink
    Images of the Professor's final fiery dance flashed across Wheldrake's mind as he snapped into consciousness. Somewhere nearby, the sound of flowing water. It was perfectly dark, but he could feel dampness in the air. By the Gods' sweet mercy, the stink! It was old and rich as if fermented into putridity over an age or more.

Shhhhrrrink

A pain; a tightness to the skin and a sting that could only be burns. Superficial, he knew. He would be in much more pain if they were worse. Still, what he wouldn't give for some light.

Shhhrink

What the hell was that sound? He knew it, but in the darkness all he saw was memories of flame and then darkness.

"Who are you?"

Wheldrake scrambled backward until his head slammed on something that *bonged* like a full bathtub.

"Who's there?" he asked, searching the dark for

anything, anything at all.

"I asked first. Who are you?"

"My name is Wheldrake."

A match flared, exposing something vaguely human and entirely hideous in the dark. A small lamp was lit.

That face. Wheldrake knew that face. At least, he knew half of it.

"Darrant? Captain Darrant?" he asked, squinting.

"I've not been called that for a long time."

Darrant was badly scarred, just as Steadfast had described. Wheldrake noticed the hand closest the lamp was missing a few digits.

"How long have you been down here?" he asked. Although he knew the answer, he knew it probably seemed longer for Darrant.

"Long enough. But not here. These are the deepest reaches of the sewer system. No one and nothing comes here."

"Except you," said Wheldrake.

"I have my reasons. As must you. I know all about you, Wheldrake. You're a famous man. Now why would someone like you be down here?" Darrant turned his eyes on Wheldrake, taking in every aspect of his stoat-like face. There was no surprise in his eyes. Wheldrake realised that Darrant had seen stranger specimens than him in his time below. It was a harrowing thought.

Shhhhrrrink. The whet stone ran along Darrant's sword. It looked extremely keen already, but Wheldrake wasn't about to question it.

Through a fog of recent trauma, surprise and utter confusion, a distant thought probed Wheldrake. Something far down, almost as far as he had come physically, wanted to surface. Something he should be noticing.

No, it wouldn't come yet. Damn.

"Do you have water?" he asked.

Darrant passed him a canteen, moving closer with

the lamp to do so. They sat in their little pond of light and shared it in silence.

Wheldrake scraped away at his brain. There was something buried there that still demanded his attention. It was on the tip of his memory, ready to teeter over into his mind. It swayed there, but still wouldn't come.

Darrant wondered what could bring Loosestrife's old assistant into his pitch domain in such a state. His clothes were charred, there were burns on his hands and soot on his face. A fire had been the beginning of his journey, then. But that didn't explain the contraption that Wheldrake had brought with him.

Finally, Darrant had to ask.

"What is that thing?"

"What thing?" asked Wheldrake.

"The machine. What does it do?"

So, Darrant has gone mad, Wheldrake thought.

"I'm sorry, I don't know what you're talking about."

"Don't test me, Wheldrake. The sewers are *my* place, and you're trespassing. I'm allowing you to stay but my patience is thin. What *is* it?"

He pointed to something over Wheldrake's shoulder.

The scientist turned.

It was a curved shape, large. He snatched Darrant's lamp and lifted it. The shape was covered in a thick layer of lichen, but beneath, in patches, the light touched metal.

Darrant spoke again, but Wheldrake didn't hear. He shoved the lamp back into Darrant's hand and began to scrabble at the slick coating on the contraption, staining his hands a deep green.

Darrant watched the mad man scratch at the brass hulk. Wheldrake hadn't brought it with him. Of course not. It was too old, too dirty. It had been here a lot longer than that. Whatever it was, a pale blue glow wavered inside. Darrant moved forward, curiosity forcing him to peer through the contraption's small window.

There was a fluid filling the tank-like device; fluid, and something else.

No, some*one*.

44

The Hunter's Staff had low ceilings, low expectations and low clientele from every corner of Greaveburn's underbelly. If there were no door, the interior would be impossible to distinguish from the street outside. Mud, blood and clotted hay covered the floor; if anyone were to scratch around they would find loose teeth. Tables from all walks of life had been collected in one place, some were fashioned from off-cuts of wood and rusty nails. Smoke billowed from the fire beneath the mantel, some of it coming into the room to join the tobacco cloud. Only the barman dared look up from his work. Making involuntary eye contact with anyone in The Hunter's Staff could be met with immediate violence, or worse, a grudge that would be repaid anytime, anywhere. Every voice was lowered to a murmur; the hum sounding like whispering madness.

"You're either very brave or very stupid, my friend."

Someone had come to sit at Lynch and Schism's table. He brought a tankard of ale. Lynch's body became tense, but he didn't strike. Lynch was an attack dog; he would only react on orders, but then it would be with the full ferocity of his nature. Schism decided to look up at their visitor, intending to threaten with a smile. After a moment of confusion, he recognised the face. "And I see it's the latter. It's been a long time, Captain."

Steadfast looked about him, to check if anyone had heard.

"Don't worry, Captain. No one cares or dares to know what we're talking about."

"They're scared I'll knife 'em," offered Lynch.

"Indeed. Now what is it we can do for you this evening?"

Steadfast looked at Schism's pale, shiny face; like grease on the moon. There was either crooked intelligence or utter insanity behind those eyes, he couldn't tell which. Casting a look at Lynch, he saw brutal stupidity. These two were the perfect combination.

"I have a job for you," said Steadfast, and drank heavily from his tankard.

"And by that draught, it's a hefty one, I presume?" said Schism.

Steadfast hated him, and that smirk of his. He'd hated him ever since he saw Abrasia leave in their custody, never to be seen again.

Abrasia. It had been so long since he'd thought of her. Each time he'd asked Wheldrake what had become of the girl he'd received the same answer. She's safe. Safe where? Only Wheldrake knew. Maybe that was for the best.

Thinking of that girl in this place seemed sacrilege. Steadfast turned his attention back to Schism. He could punch that man square in the face with little remorse. Even as Lynch beat him bloody in a room full of eye witnesses who would later plead temporary blindness, he would still feel no regret.

"The man they call Riccall, I want you to find him. Find him and kill anyone who you find to be in his company. The Broken Folk need to be culled. Those in Riccall's immediate circle are the ring leaders. Without them, the rest of the abominations will have no one to lead them and it will be a simple matter for the Guard to round them up."

Schism didn't bother to feign surprise. Work was work and, of late, the paying kind only came from the inner city.

"Payment?"

"Name it," said Steadfast.

"Ah, I see. We'll require half before the deed, half after. In this case, the conditions we find at the point of production will discern if the second half is substantially larger that the first. I feel this could be a particularly dangerous errand."

"Good," said Steadfast, and drained his rusty tankard and emptied his pocket of the cloth bag which sounded heavy when it hit the tabletop.

He stopped before leaving. He had hoped to leave it at that, to walk away before his resolve could melt.

"One more thing."

"Yes?"

"Riccall. I want him alive. Unharmed. I want him," said Steadfast.

"Ah, you wish to make an example."

Steadfast paused, his jaw muscles working.

"Yes."

45

In the cool glow of the Elixir, Abrasia floated beyond time. Her hair was a gilt seaweed mane. A strand drifted across her face, obscuring her features. Darrant's fingers stroked the glass as if to brush it aside.

The poor girl. His girl. His charge.

But alive, or so Wheldrake would have him believe. He couldn't stop smiling, shaking his head.

"We have to take her back," he said.

Wheldrake rebound his burns with a rag. He spoke through gritted teeth.

"It's not safe, Darrant. Nothing's changed. In fact, it's worse. The Cholers are everywhere, in everything and everyone. You and I; we're a minority." He thought of Steadfast for a moment, then kept on binding. "Less than that, even. We're an anomaly."

Darrant climbed down from his seat atop The Womb to perch across from Wheldrake. He tied the knot that Wheldrake was struggling with. The grip between his thumb and little finger had become surprisingly dextrous.

"Thank you," said Wheldrake.

"The rightful heir to Greaveburn's throne is in that

casket, Wheldrake. The city may be overrun by the Cholers, but Greaveburn itself is ready for her. It's sick. Tired. The time is now."

"The Cholers haven't done so badly in the public's eyes. Yes, they're tyrants. Yes, they're surely insane. And yes, the Shackles is cut off. But the former is expected, and they blame you and the Broken Folk for the rest. The Cholers gave them a cure for the Ague and brought fresh water to the whole of the city. They won't forget that in a hurry."

"No, *you* did that. So do it again. Give them something else. Something better. Something in the Glenhaven name."

Wheldrake sank into silence. He could see why the Broken Folk had followed Darrant, even to their deaths. He was compelling.

"There is something," Wheldrake began. "But it wouldn't come overnight. It would take years of building and study, and I lost all of the research in the fire."

"You mean it would give jobs to the poor and result in a brighter future if we worked together?" said Darrant.

"By the Gods, man. You're a force to be reckoned with."

Darrant's smile crept across one half of his face, so alien a sensation that he touched it.

"I used to be," he said.

"I suppose we could reinstate the homeless housing in Ginnal Avenue. Build on the Shackles and have done with the whole stinking area," said Wheldrake. "I must have had a bang on the head to even be thinking about this."

"See? It's perfect!" said Darrant.

"Hardly. We still have to get Abrasia back into the Citadel where everyone can see her. It'll be no easy feat."

"I have a man who might help. He's got me into the inner city before. Let me see him. We can do this."

"One step at a time, Darrant. Contact your…accomplice. We'll go from there."

46

"Gahk achk"

"I think you may be squeezing a little tight, Lynch"

"I'll keep going 'til his head pops off."

"How exactly do you expect to get information out of him afterward?"

The victim's swollen eyes darted between the silhouettes of his attackers. Through the gloom, only voices were clear. That was enough. Somewhere below his dangling toes was the pavement, but he had no idea where. There was just the slick cold of the wall behind him and the taste of tears. His fear was a spreading warmth. The smell of mouldy dog came from the man with knuckles like conkers.

The hand that clasped his throat loosened slightly and air whistled into his body.

Into a patch of moonlight slid the mask of Lynch. His lips were cracked, a sore on the lower; a harsh underbite, and drool on his bottom lip. The eyes were set into pools of ink that could have contained anything.

The little man whimpered.

"Don't think I'm done with you little doggy," rumbled Lynch. The man turned his head as Lynch's spittle splattered his face. "Answer the nice man's questions and I'll only think about killin' you."

"As you can see," said Schism from the dark, "my companion has issues with self-restraint. With that in mind, let's make this conversation as succinct as possible shall we? Nod if you agree."

Nod. Nod.

The little man's eyes never left Lynch's face.

"Good. Now, you know where Riccall is. Nod if that's true."

Nod.

"And you're going to tell us."

Nod.

"Good man. Lynch, I think you can let him down now."

Lynch grunted but did as he was told.

The little man folded in on himself, hitting the cobbles with a wet crunch.

"Now then, let's hear it, my friend. Let's hear it and you might just live to see the sunrise."

The little man tried to speak but his words fell dead in his mouth. He tried again, but only a squeak of shattered vocal chords came.

"Oh dear. I think you've broken him, Lynch."

"Not yet, I haven't."

"Can you write?" asked Schism.

The little man shook his head.

"Ah. Then we have a problem."

Lynch's shadow menaced. The little man tried to worm his shoulder blades into the wall, kicking with his feet in an effort to retreat. He pointed wildly to a spot on the ground.

"What's that?"

Lynch stopped.

The little man pointed again.

"The sewer, yes, we know that already," said

Schism.

"What's he doing that for?" said Lynch.

With his hand, the little man made waves.

"I have no idea. Kill him and let the Gods figure it out."

Lynch let out a chuckle and popped his knuckles. The little man shrank into a ball and tried to plead, but couldn't.

Schism's hand grasped Lynch's shoulder.

"No, wait. You, do that thing with your hand again."

The little man obliged.

"You mean 'water' don't you?"

Nodnodnod.

Water again, then a finger moving along the same imaginary line.

"I'm sorry. I don't see where you're going with this."

"He's grottin' stalling," Lynch grunted. Schism ignored him.

Water, finger. Water, and two fingers pointed downward, waggling.

"Dangle something in the water?"

Shake shake.

"No...walking! You mean walking."

Nodnodnod.

"My dear friend. I think you might have just saved your own life. Lynch, let's go." Schism moved away down the alley.

"What? What about him?" asked Lynch.

"Leave him. He's earned it."

"*Bah!*" Lynch grabbed the little man, forcing his head down onto the cobbles. "You'd better ask your lucky stars for one more favour. Make sure I never see you again."

"Lynch, come on," came Schism's voice from around the corner.

"*Bah!*"

47

A silent horde of mourners covered the burial ground's highest hill. Pale faces extended as far as the eye could see, shining in the mass of black velvet like spider's eggs.

The Archduke's coffin sat on a dais before the family mausoleum's double doors; its embroidered covering fluttered in the breeze. Stone cherubs pouted and puckered from above the mausoleum's door as if whistling. Grinda Choler stood at the head of the coffin, a veil of black lace hiding her features. At least the Archduke would be happy in a coffin. It was technically the safest place he would ever be.

All pretence had gone. Handkerchiefs remained unstained by tears. There was only dutiful and short-lived respect. The whole Choler clan were assembled for no other reason than their fear of Grinda.

The service composed by Grinda was daunting, and the priest delivered it with shaky enthusiasm. Someone nearby cleared their throat, reminding Steadfast that time was still passing in this dismal place. He shifted his weight while barely moving. The Choler standard he held never wavered. Years of guard duty had taught him something, then. It had taught him patience, too, but it was being tested.

No one noticed the beads of sweat on the poor priest's brow or the way his eyes flicked toward Grinda between every line. With the end of the eulogy in sight, he was talking faster. No one stopped him.

Steadfast looked down, across the twin hills that made up Greaveburn's necropolis. Across the small valley he could just make out a row of graves almost indistinguishable from the rest. The Glenhaven plot. Abrasia's coffin lay there, beside her father's. Two generations of Glenhavens, the last two, only empty boxes.

A black figure moved along the row. Whoever he was, Steadfast almost envied his bravery, and then corrected himself. Stupidity. To defy an invitation to the Archduke's funeral would surely lead to an untimely and slow death.

Gravel crunched under Corwater's boots; the *tack tack tack* of his cane as accompaniment.

When there had been no signs of anything interesting happening at the funeral, he'd left. There was nothing for him there. He'd never even met Legat, that he could remember. Greaveburn's nobility was possibly the loneliest place to exist. Corwater knew every name, every allegiance, but faces were rare; actions and rumours of actions defined character. News of his own roguish behaviour had certainly been spread that way. He'd seen to it himself. Something more powerful than seeing an act of rebellion was hearing of it third hand. Things grew in the telling. He'd once heard a tale about himself from a woman who didn't know who he was. He'd grown by a foot, become even more dashingly handsome, and apparently won a duel he'd never fought without drawing his sword.

Corwater smiled to himself. Sometimes, he loved

this city.

The Glenhaven plot slotted itself between those of the other nobles with little ceremony. The only difference, and only on close inspection, were the tombstones themselves. Where the palest granite was used elsewhere, marble marked the resting places of Greaveburn's rulers.

Abrasia's stone was easy to find; a single column of white marble with green tracery. It was exquisite. Corwater rested his palm against the marker's face and tried to feel something of the girl below, but he couldn't. It wasn't often he liked people. Abrasia was another of Greaveburn's upper crust that he'd never really met, but he'd loved her for her stance and her attitude. There were others that felt the same. Her name still appeared in smoke room conversation or behind clustered fans. Had she still been alive, there would surely be support for her after two years of Choler insanity. And Corwater knew the right people now. At least, he knew Happenstance and *he* knew the right people. But it was too late in the game for a total rebellion. Not enough pieces on his side of the board.

He stood up, one ankle cracking like firewood.

The coronation was only three days away and he couldn't wait. He had a big entrance planned. One that would make Grinda combust on the spot if she knew. Corwater could taste the idea like honey, and he licked at his fingers as if sampling the sweetness of it. Across the way, the funeral was breaking up. Black clad mourners moved down the hillside like treacle. Striding away, Corwater whistled between his teeth. There had to be a wake somewhere that he could hijack.

Steadfast had chosen the pallbearers himself. All of them were new to the guard so their uniforms were still serviceable. The Archduke's coffin rose as if the man inside had no weight at all. They passed beneath the mausoleum's arch, Steadfast leading the way with the Choler standard. Oil lamps gave the crypt's vault a damp light that barely cut through the shadows.

"Set him down there lads," said Steadfast, slotting the standard into a hole in the ground.

Slipping down from the Constables' shoulders, the coffin came to rest on the platform.

"That's it. You can all go. Good job boys, and remember to look sombre when you leave. If you can cry, do so. This was the ruler of all Greaveburn, and he deserves that at the very least."

They filed out, but one of them stayed.

"Doesn't it bother you, sir?" asked Maurice.

"What's that, Lieutenant?"

"Being down here, doesn't it bother you?"

Steadfast looked around at the small doors in either wall, packed with Choler bones; plaques of stone and brass bearing names he didn't know. Cobwebs smothered the ceiling like clouds.

"No," he said. "It's part of The Duty. You get along and buy those boys a drink. I'll give you the money out of petty cash when I get back tomorrow."

"Alright, sir. I'll get a couple of the lads to stand guard outside tonight once the mourners have all gone home."

"That's a good idea. You'll make sergeant soon enough. I'll use my whistle if I need help."

"Alright, sir. Goodnight."

Alone, Steadfast perched himself in an alcove nearest the door. Tucking hands into armpits, he let out a shuddering breath. It crystallised and drifted away. There was an awful draft somewhere.

He thought of the last time he'd performed the honour guard, in a place so different from this. He thought of Abrasia; the faces of Schism and his troll as they carried her away. He wondered where they were now, if the deed was done, and when he would receive Darrant.

48

"He was telling us to follow the water," said Schism. "Not that you can call it water down here."

Things bobbed in the sewer's flow, mostly submerged and obscured. The fluid bubbled and swirled, but still managed to dribble in a definite direction.

"I still don't get it." Lynch readjusted the sack over his shoulder. Glass clinked on glass.

"You don't have to. Just follow me and stay quiet."

The sack clinked gain.

"I said *quiet*."

"I'm being grottin' quiet. It's these bottles a-clatterin'."

"Well be careful with them, too. Don't break them."

Narelle squealed.

Chintz's head snapped upward. The girl was laughing. He went back to hauling his net out of the slurry. It was almost empty and didn't take much effort.

"Look at that!" shouted Narelle.

Birgit tugged on the pole, muscles in her slender arms standing out with the strain. A horse's saddle rose out of the water, shedding green sludge. The pole wobbled under the weight as Birgit swung it around to the bank.

"I wonder what happened to the rest of the horse," she said, laughing. "It still amazes me what people throw down here."

Narelle raised her crutches as high as she could, wanting to be picked up.

Birgit let out a grunt as she lifted.

"You're getting too big for all this lifting, Narelle." Narelle seemed not to notice. Birgit set her down on top of the saddle, broken little legs tucked underneath. Narelle sat up as straight as she could, Birgit rocking the saddle back and forth, and waved like she imagined princesses waved.

From her seat, Mrs Foible watched them, smiling to herself.

"Pardon me."

Mrs Foible almost fell from her stool. The voice was right over her shoulder.

A man. No, two men.

"Who are you?" she demanded.

"My name is Schism. This is my associate, Mr Lynch."

With that the bent old creature, Lynch, took a glass bottle from the sack at his feet and smashed it on the wooden railing. Liquid soaked into the wood.

"Never mind introducin' ourselves," he said. Striking a match with his haggard thumbnail, he watched the flame settle.

"Indeed. I believe my companion is about to prove that actions speak louder than words."

Lynch dropped the match. Flames spread in tongues of blue and red along the oil-soaked wood.

Mrs Foible span away from the men, hobbling toward the steps down to the sewer's side. Lynch's hand came down and grabbed hold of her shawl.

"*Chintz!*" she yelled. "*CHINTZ!*"

Chintz dropped the net and was lolloping toward Rickety Bridge before the second shout came. Mrs Foible struggled against someone he didn't recognise. The glare of spreading flames masked the offender's shape. As he moved closer, the old woman was tossed to the boards. The grinning man hopped down the steps and rose against Chintz.

"Now then, big 'un," Lynch said. "You're just what I've been waiting for."

"Narelle, stay here."

"What's happening?"

"I don't know, just stay here. I'll come back."

Birgit ran up onto Rickety Bridge. A man bent over Mrs Foible. As she watched, he placed his hat down on the floor and reached out to the old woman with a slender blade.

Birgit ran forward, yelling. Schism's head snapped upward just in time to see Birgit's boot scything toward his face. Glanced by the blow, he fell away, rolling with the momentum of the strike. Birgit ducked toward Mrs Foible, trying to drag her to her feet, but Schism was quickly up and moving back toward them, the spreading flames making his knife flash in the gloom.

Mrs Foible shoved with her feet as Birgit dragged her away by the armpits.

Chintz brought one massive hand around. Lynch took the hit, swaying on his feet.

"Grottin' bitch pup," he muttered, and dove for Chintz's waist. They fell against the wall together, Chintz's mouth opening in a yell, but no sound escaped.

Lynch dug a fist into the mute's kidneys, and

another. Winded, Chintz dropped to the stones. A kick lifted him from the floor only to slam down again.

From where Narelle sat, one side of Rickety Bridge was a clot of smoke and flickering orange light.

Chintz and another man danced around each other on the sewer's walkway, exchanging blows.

Birgit dragged something hidden by the Rickety Bridge's railing, a man in black advanced toward her. He was saying something.

Narelle whimpered as she stretched her fingers as far as they would go, gradually moving a crutch toward her. She wriggled herself free of the saddle and used wall and crutch to raise herself.

"There's no need for any of this." Schism raised his voice over the sound of cracking wood. "We can leave as quickly as we've come. All I need is information."

He held the blade between his fingers as if offering a flower.

Rickety Bridge was no place for fire. It spread through the jumble, leaping, tasting everything. Birgit's eyes darted to either side as the flames crawled toward her. A keening sound escaped the depths of her throat.

"Birgit, just go," muttered Mrs Foible.

Birgit ignored her, or didn't hear. Her eyes rolled as if trying to escape the flames reflected there.

"There's no need to be afraid. You can leave here as soon as we're done," said Schism. "Madame, I get the feeling that your attention is elsewhere. I do so hate being ignored."

He dove forward, catching Birgit by the arm. Mrs Foible fell to the ground again, her tiny feet kicked at Schism's ankles. He ducked low, cuffing the old woman about the face, knocking her unconscious. Birgit squirmed against him. Her knee came up and hit him in the thigh.

"Stand still," he said and hit her hard.

The man hit Birgit. She went limp in his arms.
"*Birgit!*"
Narelle shuffled along the path, her single crutch barely keeping her aloft. Across the sewage flow, Chintz had fallen. The other man stood over him and spat. He turned, and Narelle caught his eye.

She screamed as if his gaze had struck her, and tried to move faster.

There was no way Lynch could get to the girl across the bridge. Black smoke billowed from it, rolling in on itself when it met the sewer's ceiling. Parts of the makeshift structure were starting to peel off. The sewer swallowed them. It was no use, he'd have to go through the water.

Lynch looked down at the flow. It was faster here, but he could manage if he took it steady. He lowered himself down.

The slurry stank like warm death.

He knew very little about children and their habits. He remembered being one himself only distantly, but he *did* know that they sang like birds if you twisted them right.

"I want to know where Riccall is."

Birgit yelled, wriggled and beat at Schism. The fire was too much for her. Foam lined her lips. She was wild.

The switchblade bit into her cheek, and Birgit screamed.

"Pay attention. I want to know where Riccall is," Schism said again. "Or you'll lose the pretty side of your face as well."

"He's not here," she managed. Hot blood coursed down her neck. "The swine's not here."

"That's no way for a lady to talk, my dear. If he's

not here, then where is he?"

"I don't know. *Ow*, you're hurting my arm."

"Yes, I know."

"We don't know. We really don't know."

Chintz came through the flames and smoke like a battleship through a fog bank. Some of his suit was aflame, his face was bloodied and scorched, a faint wisp of smoke rose from his hat. His fist came down on Schism's neck.

The villain crumpled like a sack of bricks.

Chintz scooped Mrs Foible from the floor. He nudged her, shook her, and stroked her hair. She lay too still in his arms.

Birgit turned away, eyes streaming against the smoke.

Narelle's scream scraped across the air, through the crackling of the flames and the sound of Schism's half-conscious moaning.

Birgit pushed Chintz aside.

Lynch had her girl. Narelle tried to scream again but couldn't for the hand wrapped around her frail throat. Her feet dangled in the air, kicking against nothing.

Birgit darted forward. Flames were everywhere. She stopped, pushed back by the heat. Her face tingled as if in warning. She touched her scars, whimpering as if they were new.

Beyond the blaze, Narelle's eyes were starting to roll. Her little fingers slipped from where they had fought Lynch's massive fist.

Bursting through the blaze, arms across her face, Birgit landed heavy and rolled on the stone. She was up on her feet before Lynch could turn around. Then she was on his chest. Her dirty nails gouged his face. Blood was in his eyes, his mouth.

Lynch swung his arm, batting Birgit aside with Narelle's flaccid body. Both women, large and small, fell again. Narelle bounced across the ground and away. Birgit stumbled toward the girl, but Lynch rose behind her, one eye closed against the blood, one like a white hot coal. He grabbed at her clothing, dragging her away from Narelle. Birgit screamed frustration and fear.

Chintz swung himself into view, catching hold of Lynch's throat. Lynch wrapped his hands around the mute's wrist. Chintz's fist came into his face with all the force he could muster.

An eruption of crimson droplets. Again and again.

Lynch squirmed against the onslaught, feet kicking, hands catching Chintz with glancing blows. Blood speckled the dank walls of the sewer.

Everything became still.

Chintz hit Lynch's motionless husk one last time, to make sure, and let it fall into the sewer.

Birgit's fingers dug into the ground as she sought for purchase. Her thin body slid toward Narelle. With firelight flickering across the girl's frame, it was impossible to tell if she was breathing.

Birgit could finally touch her.

Beneath her palm, Narelle was cold, tacky with sweat.

"Narelle. Narelle?"

The girl lunged, her arms wrapped around Birgit's neck. They slid against the wall in a heap. Birgit folded over Mrs Foible's body, Narelle still in her arms; tears spread evenly between gratitude and grief.

With a groan like the last breath of a dragon, Rickety Bridge buckled. Shards of wood and a host of rubbish fell into the water below, bearing Schism's body with it. A splash, the hiss of doused flame, and the sound of sobs that echoed away.

49

Bunting swung from rooftop to rooftop; black, purple and gold vines in a forest of stone. Against a dense grey sky, the decorations seemed even more drab.

Steadfast turned into the street, his boots splashing in last night's rain.

People flooded the streets, even more than usual. Baskets, chairs, decorations, and a ladder floated above their heads. A pair of women in white caps wove their way past Steadfast with a roll of cloth between them. He was jostled aside and rebounded from a baker, apron and all, carrying a basket of bread rolls. A group of children swarmed, brushing his uniform in their haste. On reflex, Steadfast checked his pockets. Nothing was stolen.

At either side of the pavement, men stood on ladders hoisting a banner into place; "Long Live the Queen". As one tugged, the other almost fell. To the casual observer, it was obvious that the banner wouldn't stretch the width of the street. Steadfast hurried past so that he wouldn't have to deal with whoever fell first.

Another street, more decorations, more people bustling to and fro. He swerved between them unseen. Not one of the Greaveburners smiled or chatted. This was the feverish work of ants trying to appease a hungry Queen.

Steadfast's thoughts turned to Lynch and Schism.

It had been three days since The Hunter's Staff and he'd heard nothing. Maybe Darrant had taken himself away, maybe out of Greaveburn entirely, or had crawled into a hole to die like an ailing cat. With Grinda Choler's coronation tomorrow, Steadfast's nerves span like a coin on its edge, to either land on insanity or murder.

Large ceramic pots stood at intervals, marking an aisle toward the Citadel. In each pot was a tower of pale flowers footed by roses. In the crowd, Steadfast spotted the Inspectors' long black coats. They stood still, allowing the people to flow around them. Only their heads swung this way and that, like hanged corpses. He spotted Cawber among them. If the Chief Inspector hadn't turned his way, Steadfast would have escaped without speaking. Unfortunately, Cawber missed nothing.

"Checking up on me, Captain?" asked Cawber. He had a nasty habit of pumping his fists as if constantly spoiling for a fight. Or it could have been some nervous gesture, but Steadfast doubted it.

"Do I need to?"

"Of course not," Cawber sneered. "Just surprised to see you here with so many preparations to make. Can her soon-to-be-Majesty spare you?"

"I'll be reporting to her soon enough. How go the interrogations?"

"From the Galleria theft? Done. It wasn't hard to break the Broken a little bit more." The Inspector chuckled. Steadfast fought to keep his lunch in his stomach. To save speaking, he nodded. Cawber looked Steadfast up and down. "Don't you have some buttons to polish before the ceremony?"

Steadfast tugged his uniform straight. His teeth were pressed so tightly together that his jaw ached. He spotted Sergeant Barghest stood behind one of the large flower pots, smoking a cigarette. Thank the Gods. With a curt nod to Cawber, Steadfast made for his Sergeant.

"How are the preparations, Sergeant?" He checked over his shoulder. Cawber took another few seconds to look away.

"Not so bad, sir. I think we'll be mostly done by tonight. Then we just have to wait for the food to arrive tomorrow morning. Looks like it'll be a real party," said Barghest. He took the limp cigarette from his lips and squeezed the end. The stub disappeared into his pocket.

"Was that sarcasm, Sergeant?"

"None intended, sir. Just an observation."

"I find it's best not to observe too much around here, Barghest. Seeing things gets you in trouble. Just keep your eyes open for anyone who shouldn't be here, and otherwise keep them closed, alright?"

"You got it, sir. Still, with so many people milling around, it's hard to tell who should be here and who shouldn't."

Steadfast looked around him. Barghest was right. He didn't know a single scurrying face. Anyone could be anyone, or no one. How could Schism and his dog find Darrant if he was already there?

50

Darrant and Wheldrake moved through midnight as if it belonged to them.

Everything was reduced to shades and suggestions by the fog. Somewhere nearby, cattle lowed. This was the only time of any day when the streets of Greaveburn were silent. The alehouses and taverns were closed, their patrons were sleeping it off in whatever cot or gutter they could find. Soon, the Warehouse District would wake and begin the trading day. By then, the duo and Abrasia would be long gone.

Rattling its bridle, the cart horse pawed the ground. It nuzzled a weed springing through the cobbles. Inside a crate, The Womb and Abrasia were hoisted up onto the cart's rear. Wheldrake did most of the lifting.

"How do you do that?" asked Darrant, his breathing heavy.

Wheldrake hopped down and dusted off his new suit. "I suppose I'm built for it. Where did you get these clothes?"

"I told you, I have an informant. He smuggles things out of the inner city. I told him we would need clothes and a cart, he makes sure they're in the right place at the right time."

"Handy," said Wheldrake.

In the moonlight, Darrant looked almost his old self. His hair was blonde once again, suit clean and fitted. His sword belt, fashioned from a strap of crocodile skin, held Steadfast's sword. If only for his face and the hollow fingers of a glove, time might have been be reversed.

"Have you *bathed*?" asked Wheldrake.

"There was a trough in the barn over there. I could hardly let them smell us coming could I?"

They climbed into the cart and Darrant shook the reins.

The cart rolled forward, horse puffing against The Womb's weight.

If the Citadel was Greaveburn's brain, and the sewer its bowels, then the Warehouse District was the stomach. Acres of wooden buildings housed livestock, stored grains, and gave workshops to tanners and liveries that weren't welcome in the Artisan's quarter. The cart rolled past stable, abattoir and livery; the lifecycle of Greaveburn's beasts. Peeking above the rest of the buildings, extending chimneys like smoking cigars, Grissam's Glue Factory made the best of what was left.

They followed the ruts in Thribald Lane until the Warehouses were behind them. There was an hour or more of driving before they ducked beneath the Belfry's legs and curled around to the west. They saw only one person, a blacksmith. Coal-streaked muscles bunched as he pumped amber light from his furnace. He stopped to wipe his brow and gave the conspirators a nod.

Before reaching the inner city's eastern gate, Darrant drew to a halt.

"What are we waiting for?" asked Wheldrake.

"Our third member."

"You didn't say anything about this, Darrant."

"My accomplice's demands were simple. He would get us what we need to smuggle Abrasia into the Citadel on the condition that he came with us. I saw no harm in it. An extra sword arm will come in handy," said Darrant, searching the shadows.

"How do you know we can trust him? If he's a noble, it could be a trap. If Abrasia is found by the Cholers before we can unveil her, they'll kill her for good. A lot of people have to see her all at once if this is to work."

"The plan still stands. Now let it be. I trust him, that's enough."

"Do you really?" The voice came out of the dark, sharp enough to make even Wheldrake jump.

Corwater stepped out of the shadows.

"Do I what?" asked Darrant.

Wheldrake sat in silence, watching them talk. He'd never seen the third man before. He was slick in movement and appearance; oil personified.

"Trust me," said Corwater. A smile greased his face.

"No," replied Darrant without pausing. "Now let's get a move on before we're seen."

Corwater smiled: "Splendid."

The cart rolled on.

"My dear fellow," said Corwater, swaying atop the crate. "I hope you don't mind me saying, but you have a most singular appearance."

Wheldrake turned to Corwater, then glanced at Darrant.

"Between the three of us," he said. "I'd say *you* were the odd one out."

Corwater chuckled. "I suppose you're right. But someone has to be the public face of any endeavour."

As dawn leaked over the horizon, row upon row of guards stood to attention in the yard.

Steadfast walked along the front row, past his sergeants. He found a point somewhere in the centre of the row and stopped, facing them all. Barghest stood directly in front of him. Steadfast could smell the scent of age coming from him; a faint musk of urine and stale cigarette smoke.

"Good morning," said Steadfast. "You all know what today is. You know your duties and your posts. I expect great things from all of you. I expect you to stand to attention as if your spines are fused, your eyes to be on stalks, and your scabbards to be loose. This is a time of great stress for Greaveburn, and incompetence is not an option. Anyone who lets me down will get more than relief of their duties.

"Make no mistake, boys. The Inspectors and their men will be everywhere, and they will be watching you as closely as any other. They hate you. Every one of you. They have her Majesty's favour and as such we are to follow their lead. They are *experts* in spotting revolutionaries. They can sniff them like dogs.

"But, when the carriage loses its wheels, dogs get crushed underneath. Should anything go wrong; should any insurgents make a strike against her Majesty, then you will listen to the instructions of your sergeant above any other.

"Dismissed."

The sergeants saluted and turned about like tin solders. They began to bark orders, each to their own company. Movement in the ranks. Dark blue uniforms spread over the cobbled yard like royal blood.

The Eastern Gate was closed. After too many harsh winters, the immense hinges had become great scabs of iron. No one had seen fit to fix them. Darrant and his militia looped around to the south. Skirting the inner city wall, they passed through the Labyrinth, an area of nameless streets so narrow that the cart brushed buildings on either side. Three stories above, the rooftops almost touched, blocking out the rising dawn.

More carts and trailers joined them as they met Southgate Avenue, until they were just another market-bound cart in the crowd. Feathers from excitable chickens in a neighbouring cart spiralled like snowflakes. Corwater brushed them from his jacket with a grunt. Stood in the traffic, they watched as poles were shoved skyward, lifting the spice market's cloth ceiling. Despite the coronation, trade went ahead; too much would perish and be wasted if it didn't. Bartering would officially stop at midday when the coronation began. Unofficially, it would carry on.

The traffic crawled forward. Carts peeled off and became stalls, some continued through the Southern Gate bound for inner city festivities. Two straight-backed young corporals full of coffee and new-job enthusiasm barred the way. A third man stood behind them smoking a cigarette, a burst of silver on his black jacket. Darrant eyed him. The face was familiar.

He lowered his chin from the Chief Inspector's gaze, tucking his face further into the hood he wore for just such an occasion.

The taller of the young guards stepped forward, hand raised.

"What are you carrying?" he demanded, lifting his eyes over the cart's side to regard the crate.

"Wine," said Corwater. "From the Choler vaults."

He pointed to a seal stamped on the side, one he'd made sure was there.

"Where are you headed?"

"The Citadel, of course. Who else would be drinking the Queen's wine?" Corwater looked over the guard's shoulder to address the man in black. "I trust you have no issues with allowing us access, Inspector…?"

The Inspector crushed out the cigarette with his boot and, smoothing back his hair, stepped forward. Both guards retreated.

"*Chief* Inspector. Cawber," he said. He started

toward Darrant and Wheldrake.

Corwater intervened, physically stepping in front of the man.

"I apologise, Chief Inspector. I don't believe I've had the pleasure."

Cawber looked at Corwater's extended hand as if it were gangrenous.

"No. You haven't," he said. "And pray you never need to."

"Of course," said Corwater. "Well, I'll be sure to report your diligence to her Majesty at the earliest opportunity. I'm certain she will be thrilled that her new policemen are so efficient."

Cawber finally looked at Corwater. His eyes were slits, as if peering through smoke.

"Will she, indeed?"

"I'm certain of it."

Cawber took one last look at the men in the cart, or what he could see of them over Corwater's shoulder.

"Do you purposefully collect the most repulsive servants out of some misguided charity, or was it bad luck that brought these two into your employ?" said Cawber. Wheldrake met his eye and smiled. Cawber averted his gaze.

"Let them through," he said.

Corwater thanked him and turned away. Wheldrake was almost pinning Darrant into his seat.

"Not today, Darrant. Not today," whispered Wheldrake.

"Let's be away as quick as we can, eh gentlemen?" said Corwater, taking his perch.

Cluracan was ready for his cot. He swung aside the telescope, pinching the bridge of his nose.

When the sun came up, his telescope was useless. There was nothing but humility to be learnt from staring at the sun. While the stars whispered futures, the sun guarded its secrets jealously.

Through the thin glass of his tower, Cluracan heard a shout from the street below. He moved over and peered out. Only the back of the citadel could be seen from the palace, but the streets were hung with spider webs of gold and purple. People scurried like beetles, arms laden with nothing Cluracan could make out.

"Long live the queen," he said to himself.

"Cawber," muttered Darrant. "Chief Inspector? Chief piss-ant, more like."

His companions ignored him as he continued to mutter curses and vows to endanger the Chief Inspector's life in specific ways.

They were close.

The Citadel rose above the rooftops only a few streets away; its eye still bandaged with wood. Darrant was glad. If there was one thing he couldn't stand, it was being beneath that multicoloured magnifying glass. He'd always felt the heat of it, like a beetle with the sun focused on its back.

They turned down the aisle of flowers that led to the Citadel's doors. Some of the blooms had wilted overnight, and a feverish team of gardeners tended the displays with heavy gloves. A bee struggled through the air. It had been so long since seasons were important to Darrant. The realisation that summer was approaching rose like some childhood memory. Soon the smell of grass would be everywhere, and great clouds of blossom would lift from the Common on warm breezes to be carried out over the city. There would be the festival of kites. He'd always enjoyed that. He wondered if he'd see it.

"Hold!"

Darrant felt Wheldrake's hand grab his arm and he drew up sharply on the reins. The cart jerked to a stop, the horse grinding its hooves. A guard stood in their path.

"You daft inbred," yelled the guard. "Pay attention

when you're driving that thing!"

Corwater sighed, and leapt down from the cart once more.

Wheldrake looked to Darrant as Corwater moved away to negotiate with the guard.

"What's wrong with you?"

"Nothing. I got distracted, that's all."

"That's not encouraging, Darrant."

Darrant ignored him.

"I've told the sergeant about the wine. A very rare and fine vintage," said Corwater, then dropped his voice. "He's lending us six of his men to carry Abrasia inside. The crate will be placed in the cellars with orders not to touch it until I say so."

"Surely he's kidding," said Wheldrake.

"Not at all. Why carry it when we can have the guards do it? And who is going to stop a group of trained guards from entering the Citadel?" said Corwater, almost shivering with his own ingenuity.

"Rein in your humour, Corwater," said Darrant. "This isn't a joke to anyone but you."

51

Grinda stood before her reflection. She raised her chin, allowing a smile like cracked earth. A torrent of black and brown fur flowed around her. Frina buzzed, toying with the white pelt of some other animal that hung around her mother's shoulders.

"Remember your lines, Mother?"

"Of course," said Grinda. "Whenever the priest stops for breath, I say 'I will'."

"I will, I will, I *do* and then I will," said Frina. "That's how it has to go."

"Yes, yes, I will, I will."

"I do."

"I *will*. Stop playing with that will you?"

She snatched the collar from her daughter, applying a silver brooch bearing the Greaveburn 'G' with a ruby at its centre.

There was barely enough room in the chamber for mother and daughter. When Ayles entered, it became even more crowded.

"They're nearly ready, Mother."

"Good. How is the congregation?"

"Enormous," said Ayles. "They're saying they might

have to leave the doors open so that everyone can get in."

"Out of the question. Tell them whoever can't fit doesn't need to be there. I'm not having peasants gazing in from the streets."

"Of course, Mother, I'll tell them." Ayles bustled away, sneering at Frina before leaving.

"What does it feel like, Mother?" asked Frina, daring to approach again. She fluffed the fur collar, picking stray strands from the darker material.

"What?"

"Being Queen. What does it feel like?"

"Ask me again in an hour and I'll tell you."

Everything was ready.

The priest was in place, the congregation seated. It was Steadfast's job to escort Her future Majesty to the ceremony. Although it was close, Steadfast managed to make his trip to the anteroom slower. He told himself it was to give Grinda time to prepare herself.

Grinda had been ready for this for decades.

The Citadel's inner halls were dark. There were no windows and lanterns were sparse. Steadfast walked the dead centre of the corridor, his head swinging side to side, checking doorways and alcoves for movement. Sweat seemed to coat his skin constantly nowadays, like he'd devolved into a toad. Eating, sleeping, in the bath, he carried a bundle of handkerchiefs everywhere he went. Taking one out of his uniform now, he realised that it was already sodden and groaned. He'd hoped that everything would be over by the coronation; Darrant, his Broken Folk rebellion. He wanted Darrant safe in a cell. Instead, he was free, or dead. Steadfast knew Darrant would try again, even if it were the latter.

A door burst open to his right. Steadfast span, pressing his back to the wall.

A pair of maids came into the hall, arms laden with

white linen. They snickered to each other and chatted as they walked away.

Steadfast forced his sword hand to loosen, his heart to slow, his lungs to breathe.

Up ahead, a Constable guarded the junction of two corridors.

"Captain?" he called. "Sir, are you alright?"

"Fine," managed Steadfast. "I'm fine, get back to your post."

Steadfast adjusted his jacket, sword belt, and helmet before moving along. He passed the Constable without making eye contact.

The moan and crack of splintering wood.

The sound echoed through the citadel's cellars. Darrant wandered along the shelves, scraping aside curtains of cobweb. Sliding a magnum from the shelf, he wiped the bottle with his glove and lifted the hand-written label to the light. 408. That couldn't be the year. It would mean that the bottle was sealed before the known records of Greaveburn ever began. Darrant thumbed the cork. The scent was heavy like cough syrup. Tucking it under his arm, Darrant ducked beneath a low stone arch and into the chamber where Wheldrake worked.

The crate lay on the floor. Wheldrake attacked it with his crowbar, pounding at the top panel. When that didn't work, he dropped it and used his hands. Wood pried from wood, nails parted like crocodile teeth.

Darrant sat nearby, watching. There was nothing he could do that Wheldrake couldn't manage himself. He sharpened his sword to pass the time.

"Corwater should be in position," he said.

Wheldrake didn't answer, but slid a panel aside. Lantern light heliographed from The Womb's brass casing. Pale blue light flowed inside.

"What now?" asked Darrant.

"Now we open it, and pray to the Gods for some luck."

"How long will it take?"

"Not long, but it has to be done right. Help me with the sides."

The wood fell away, and Wheldrake moved to the foot of The Womb. Darrant watched as if he understood what was happening. Wheldrake strained against a valve. A small plate rotated and the Elixir began to pour out onto the floor. From inside The Womb, the *gloig gloig gloig* of air replacing fluid.

"Now what?" asked Darrant. His fingers caressed the brass hulk as if trailing through water.

"We wait."

"I suppose we have time for a drink." Darrant picked up the aired bottle of wine and offered it.

"I don't drink," said Wheldrake.

"This could be the oldest bottle of wine in Greaveburn history. Drink it."

Wheldrake took the bottle, sniffed, and took a mouthful.

"By the Gods," he wheezed.

"Good?"

Wheldrake shook his head, and passed the bottle anyway.

Darrant drank like a man on the brink of death.

52

The Citadel's throne room was trefoil in design; the congregation made up two sections, the third an aisle of deep red carpet leading to the throne's platform. Great chandeliers hung in the vault like glowing lace.

A soft buzz of conversation filled the hall; the whispering of hourglass sand. The nobles present shuffled and strained. Grinda was keeping them waiting. With the greater public doors closed, all eyes were trained on the archway at the furthest end of the red aisle.

Steadfast stood just beyond that arch, Grinda behind him, Frina and Ayles in her wake. Checking the Cholers were ready, he stepped into the light.

Wood scraped on stone as the congregation rose.

Steadfast always felt as if he couldn't walk properly at times like this, as if he were stumbling under the weight of gazes. He straightened his back beyond comfortable and strode slowly forward. His legs felt like someone had replaced his knees with cogs, making his body sway like a pendulum. The brush of Grinda's fur cloak on the carpet sounded like the breath of a predator over his shoulder. His hackles rose.

Stopping before the platform, Steadfast stepped aside, allowing Grinda and the girls to pass him. They took the platform steps, rounded the throne. Grinda's knees groaned as she knelt before the priest, lowering one leg at a time. Frina and Ayles moved off to one side.

"All present!" began the priest after a coughing start. "Bear witness to the passage of fealty upon this woman of Greaveburn-"

For Grinda, head bowed, his voice faded away. A part of her waited for the silence which she would fill with predetermined answers; a larger part celebrated her rise to incontestable power. It was all she could do not to grin.

Through her thoughts, she noticed silence from the priest.

"I will," she said, and his voice continued.

Now all she had to do was avoid going insane like Legat. Of all the Cholers, although he had been rightful heir, she had never-

"I will."

-trusted him fully. He'd had too much of a conscience, despite his upbringing.

"I do."

The priest didn't speak again.

"I do," she said, a little louder.

No answer.

Grinda looked up.

The priest wasn't even looking at her. He gawped at something beyond the congregation. The whole assembly was looking away from her, to the large doors at the end of the hall.

At the other end of the throne room, Wheldrake shouldered wood, trapping a guard's arm between the huge doors. A crunch of bone meant there was no doubt that it was broken. The arm withdrew with a scream and Wheldrake shoved, hefting a heavy bar into place. Blood stained his lip. Wiping it away only smeared it across his chin.

Darrant strode out between the rising banks of nobles. Every one of them craned to see who this intruder was while making no move to stop him. In his arms was draped a girl fashioned from silk, a slender arm hooked around his neck. She dripped water as if he'd saved her from drowning. Although her face was buried in Darrant's shirt, it was obvious who the girl was from the golden cascade of hair that nearly brushed the floor.

The gasping masses seemed to draw all the air out of the room.

Grinda grabbed at the priest's robes, almost dragging him to the ground as she rose.

She squinted down the aisle. Someone was coming. He was carrying something.

"Who is it?" she demanded of the priest. "Who *is* it?"

"Beg your pardon, my lady," said the priest. "But I don't know."

"Steadfast! Guards!"

Steadfast, waiting out of sight, peered from behind the throne.

He saw Darrant.

Saw Abrasia.

Saw Wheldrake in their wake.

Grinda was yelling and stamping her feet. Frina and Ayles had joined her on the platform, grasping at each other and whining.

Steadfast barely noticed them.

Three guards ran into the hall from the other direction and stopped dead.

Steadfast looked at them for a moment, not recognising their uniforms or knowing why they stared at him.

He looked back at Darrant, and then to his guards,

and his brain whirred into gear.

"Stop them, then!" he finally yelled. "Stop them! Save the girl!"

"What *girl?*" yelled Grinda, and cawed with frustration.

Steadfast barged past on his way to intercept Darrant, knocking the old crone aside. Frina and Ayles tried to catch Grinda as she fell, but there was a wet thump as her porcelain head cracked on the throne's furled arm.

"They're coming," said Wheldrake.

"I know."

In Darrant's arms, Abrasia moaned. The guards came down the aisle at full speed, swords drawn. The largest of the three went sprawling across the flagstones. Corwater withdrew his boot and emerged from the congregation, smiling; a thin blade slid from his cane. The second guard was already past him, but the third came too fast to stop. Corwater sidestepped him and laid open his arm. The guard's sword thudded on the carpet.

The second guard made it to Darrant, and stopped.

"Stop what you're doing and lay the girl down on the ground," said the guard. He was nothing more than a boy. Darrant could see that he'd had a hopeful shave this morning. His cheeks were irritated red, but baby smooth.

Darrant kept on walking.

"I said stop, or I'll have to use force."

The young guard was trying to negotiate with Darrant.

"Don't talk to him, arrest him!" Steadfast yelled. He stood on the lowest step of the platform, his feet bolted in place.

From behind him came the mewling of Frina and Ayles as they tended to their mother. A trickle of Grinda's blood flowed down the throne. More stained

Frina's hands as she held her mother's head.

Ayles was making a keening sound at the back of her throat.

Frina could only shout at Steadfast's back:

"She's dead! She's dead! You killed her!"

Corwater stepped in front of the guard, barring his way. Blood ran down the guard's arm, making the blue of his uniform darker. Sweat dribbled down his face, dripping from the coarse growth on his chin.

"Who the hell are you?" asked Constable Stubble.

"I'm almost offended." Corwater smiled to himself. It was possible he was enjoying this a little too much.

"Out of my way you snot-nosed prig," said the guard, making to move past.

Corwater pressed the tip of his sword against the guard's uniform.

"I'm sure you don't understand what's happening. So you'll just have to trust me when I say that it's for the best. I suggest you turn around and go back the way you came."

The guard smiled at something over Corwater's shoulder and lowered his sword.

"No, I'd suggest *you* turn around."

Corwater felt the hot breath of another assailant on the back of his neck.

"Ah."

"Step aside, boy. You don't know what you're dealing with," said Darrant.

In the full light, Darrant's scars were even more hideous. The young guard's Adam's apple disappeared, and returned. He licked his lips.

"You're Riccall aren't you?" he said.

"I was."

"And that's Lady Abrasia, back from the dead?"

Darrant blinked, and said:

"Yes."

The young guard lowered his sword.

"My Mam said she'd come back."

"Your mother is an astute woman," interrupted Wheldrake. He looked over his shoulder to where the main doors were straining on their hinges. The muffled sound of effort came from the other side. "Do you think we can hurry?"

"My Mam says she's the rightful heir to Greaveburn, and that the Cholers killed her."

"Your Mam certainly has a lot to say for herself," muttered Wheldrake.

Darrant stayed silent.

Somewhere behind, wood was buckling.

The young guard looked back toward the throne, where Steadfast stood aghast.

"I want to do the right thing," said the boy, mostly to himself.

"I think you already are," offered Darrant. "Why don't you go home and tell your Mam that you've seen Lady Abrasia and she's alive. Tell her what's happening."

"She'll say I'm mad."

"She'll believe you soon enough," said Darrant. "You don't have to be here, Son."

The young guard's eyes wavered. He wiped his cheek.

Wheldrake moved to let the boy past.

The tripped guard picked himself up. He was enormous. Strands stood out in his thick neck, veins pulsed in his arms. He swung his sword at neck height.

Corwater ducked Bullneck's swipe, only to be presented with the other assailant. Constable Stubble, arm clasped to his side, wielded his sword in the wrong hand. Spinning, Corwater countered a clumsy thrust and kicked him in the stomach. Bullneck lunged over his partner's back, catching Corwater in the shoulder with the tip of his blade. The noble stumbled backward, spare hand clutching at oozing cloth. Stubble swung for Corwater's leg, knocking him to the ground, and Bullneck was ready, sword raised, to cleave him in two.

Bullneck's face snapped to the side, as an unexpected fist cracked his chin. The guard's knees buckled. Lord Happenstance span around, picking up his chair and cracked Stubble over the back with it.

Happenstance leant over Corwater, rubbing his fist. It felt like Bullneck's chin had broken his hand.

"You're bleeding," he said.

Blood seeped through Corwater's jacket. He could feel its warmth running down his body beneath the shirt.

"Nothing a good tailor won't fix," he said. "Help me up."

"Does it hurt?" asked Lord Happenstance. He strained against the youth's weight.

"Yes."

"I thought it might."

One assisted by the other, they followed Darrant toward the throne.

Steadfast couldn't take everything in.

Darrant was drawing closer, three companions in his wake, Abrasia in his arms, and no one was trying to stop them.

The priest appeared at his shoulder:

"Captain, shouldn't you do something? I think Lady Choler may be...but, I can't be sure."

"Stop whittling. Get out of my way." Steadfast shoved the old priest aside.

"No wonder the Gods frown on you, Enoch," said Darrant. "That's no way to treat a priest."

He stood on the step below Steadfast.

Abrasia was stirring. She was alive. If only he could get her away from Darrant.

"Give the girl to me, Darrant. There's no need for

her to be harmed. You're here for me, so let's keep it that way."

"You idiot," said Darrant. "She was your charge, Enoch, and not only were you incapable of protecting her, but then you lost her. I won't give her up again."

Guards flooded the hall at the furthest end. Corwater, Wheldrake and Happenstance made a semicircle behind Darrant.

"Steadfast-" said Wheldrake.

"Shut up, traitor," said Steadfast.

"I think 'traitor' is the right word," said Darrant. "But you have the wrong person."

He stepped forward.

Abrasia's eyes were fluttering.

"Stop!" Steadfast dropped back. Drawing his sword, he held its wavering tip toward Darrant. He removed his helmet, and let it thud to the ground. "You're insane, Darrant. You've gone berserk, and you don't know when you're hurting people. I won't let you harm Abrasia."

"Alright, Steadfast."

Darrant slid Abrasia into Wheldrake's arms. When he drew his sword, Steadfast's eyes widened. The hilt had been fixed, the grip was different, but he recognised his own weapon. Darrant slid his partial hand into the strap he'd fashioned.

"I've been looking forward to this," he said.

Backed by hundreds of rapt nobles and guards, Darrant and Steadfast clashed swords for the first time. Steadfast was instantly on the defensive, Darrant delivering calculated blows to his blade. Steadfast tried to counter but was recoiled by Darrant's experienced hand. Steadfast ducked backward to give himself room, and used his superior weight against Darrant's skill.

Darrant's sword slid along Steadfast's, lodging at the hilt. They pressed each other, faces inches apart. Both breathed heavily. Darrant was tiring quicker than he'd hoped. Steadfast could see an opening.

Shoving Darrant away, he followed swiftly with hammering blows. Darrant's arm seemed to be buckling, the pressure dropping him to his knees. Steadfast came for one final strike to knock Darrant's sword from his hand.

Darrant parried wildly, and thrust upward.

The sword jerked out of Steadfast's hand.

He was off balance and falling.

"Steadfast?"

Darrant sprawled across the floor, Steadfast pressing him down.

"Steadfast?"

He rolled himself, moving Steadfast aside, and revealing where the sword pierced his friend's chest.

"Gods," whispered Darrant. Steadfast's blood was on his jacket, his shirt; his hands.

Wheldrake was beside him, tearing open Steadfast's uniform.

"I'm sorry," said Darrant.

"For what?" asked Wheldrake.

"I wasn't talking to you."

They sat for a while, staring down at the face of their friend. Steadfast looked past them; toward the ceiling, the clouds and maybe even the Gods beyond.

People were already starting to mill around as if a play had ended. Some stood in groups chunnering and mumbling between themselves. The guards ushered people out of the hall in orderly fashion. This was the Greaveburn that Darrant wanted to change. This apathy.

Darrant stood in one sweeping motion, propelling himself upward. A tear fell, rolling through scars and rivulets of flesh. Looking out over the congregation, he opened his mouth to speak; to shout. A sea of heads, and not one of them understood. Not in any way that mattered. Steadfast lay dead. Lord Happenstance held the rightful Queen of Greaveburn in his arms like a slumbering child and the audience were indifferent. He wanted to yell, to make them recognize what had been lost and gained. But nothing would come. Nothing that wouldn't be a waste of breath. Greaveburn continued as it always had, barely paying attention to itself. No single act was ever going to change that.

Happenstance stood, Abrasia curled against him, and Corwater bleeding happily at his feet. As he approached, Darrant heard their conversation:

"Because I'm a selfish, horrible man and I wanted the glory all to myself," said Corwater. He laughed, and winced. "Ow."

"You didn't think I could manage it did you? You think I'm too old," said Happenstance.

"Nothing of the sort, my Lord. But I had a hard enough time getting Darrant to let me tag along, never mind you."

Darrant held out his hands to Happenstance: "I'll take her now."

Abrasia rolled into his arms like she belonged there.

He moved across the platform, ignored by all except his companions.

Abrasia slid down into the throne, shivering against the cold. Darrant draped his jacket over her shoulders. She blinked like a newborn and tried to speak, but her voice came weak.

"It's alright," said Darrant. When he touched her hand, she saw him for the first time.

"Darrant?" she said. "You look terrible."

53

"‐ ommitted to the ground. Let all gathered remember Enoch Steadfast. Captain of the Guard and protector of Her Majesty, Abrasia."

A single trumpet blew a somber melody as the coffin descended into the ground.

The crowd dispersed, people drifting down the hill in all directions; all wearing creams and greens that shone in the cool spring sun.

Darrant knelt before Abrasia's wheelchair and reset her feet on their rest. Its engine *phut-phut-phut*ted at her back.

"I suppose I have to get used to people doing that," said Abrasia.

"Wheldrake said there's a chance you might walk yet," said Darrant.

"Yes, he's such a wonderful liar."

Darrant went to take the handles of Abrasia's chair, but she steered it away, releasing the steam with one hand and steering with the other as they moved along the path. She was grinning. Darrant hoped the novelty of the chair would never wear off almost as much as he was certain that she would come to abhor it.

"I take it the mask is staying?" continued Abrasia.

"Yes," said Darrant. He touched the ivory half-mask absently. "Unless I want to scare the new recruits. Then I leave it on my desk. Now, smile. Here come your subjects."

A procession of mourners led back toward the Citadel on foot. Every Greaveburner was on the streets, choking every inch of cobble, dressed in every shade from brown to cream. In the crowd, Darrant could make out the shapes and faces of Broken Folk he once knew.

Passing through the square that had swallowed Darrant so long ago, Corwater came out of the crowd. He bowed before stepping in time beside them.

"Your Majesty. Darrant."

"Good morning, Corwater," said Abrasia. Darrant nodded.

"I was wondering if you knew the whereabouts of Wheldrake? I haven't seen him."

"Neither have I," said Darrant. "I think he's throwing himself into his work. He says the eel's power could bring light to the inner city in a year or so with the right start."

"That will certainly be a sight," said Corwater.

"Yes, it will."

When silence fell between them, Corwater tried to fill it.

"The physician assures me that Grinda isn't close to imminent death, although they don't know how serious the blow to her head will prove to be. I doubt she'll be having any lengthy conversations for quite some time. Frina and Ayles are arguing over who will succeed her as head of the Choler family."

Darrant's mind seemed to be elsewhere. He scoured the crowds.

"Corwater, will you escort Abrasia?" he said.

"Of course."

"And where do you think you're going?" asked Abrasia.

"I'm sorry?"

"Don't think I'm letting you out of my sight, Darrant," said Abrasia. She had her smile back. "You've caused my city a lot of trouble in the last few years, even if I wasn't awake to witness it. I want you where I can see you at all times."

"I'll meet you shortly," he managed a smile. "I think I just saw someone I used to know."

Birgit stood with her arms folded, Chintz at her back with Narelle perched on his shoulders. As Darrant approached, Narelle scowled. Chintz simply looked away.

"What happened to your face?" asked Darrant.

"You know," said Birgit.

"I mean your cheek."

Birgit touched the stitches where Schism had cut her.

"Someone came looking for you," she said.

"I'm sorry," he said, massaging his brow. It seemed there was no end to the side effects of his crusade. He looked around. "Mrs Foible?"

"Dead."

Darrant lowered his chin.

He looked away, watching the procession disappear inside the Citadel. Nearby a quartet busked with fiddles and drums. A street merchant walked by with steaming, paper-wrapped sausages in a tray. Greaveburn continued.

"Come with me," Darrant said.

"Where?" asked Birgit.

"Everyone in the Shackles, and all of the Broken Folk, they're being given a place. I can find somewhere for the three of you."

"It's the least you could do," said Birgit. "But, no. We have somewhere already. We've bartered passage out of the city. The trade route opens tomorrow and we'll be on the first cart."

"You're leaving for Vale?"

"Yes. It'll be better there." She reached up and stroked Narelle's hair. "This one deserves sky and flowers."

"It will be better here soon," said Darrant, but he couldn't look her straight in the eye.

Birgit shook her head at him, just like Mrs Foible always had.

"Greaveburn will be what it always has been. New paint doesn't change the wall."

Unsure of what else he could say, Darrant walked away.

Epilogue

Spring and summer courted briefly. On the Common, kites in their hundreds blotted out the sun. The swamp vines of eastern Greaveburn flowered, turning the streets into carpets of pink and white. Clouds of blossom blew out over the city. Trees deepened to ochre. Winter came harsh and white, clouds laying low over the smoking rooftops. The Shackles became a ghost town, became a field, became a memory.

And all across Greaveburn, as night fell, lights twinkled as if reflecting the sky.

Author Bio

By day Craig is a mild mannered Nurse from Doncaster, UK. By night (or any time he gets a few minutes to himself) he writes Speculative Fiction. He's been tackling short stories since late 2008. Since then his credits have included *New Horizons* (The British Fantasy Society), *Murky Depths* and the anthologies of Misanthrope Press and Pill Hill Press. He hopes you enjoy this book, and that he'll see you hovering over another of his pages in the near future.

Contact the author here:
www.craighallam.wordpress.com

Here: craighallam@live.com

Or here on Twitter: @craighallam84